CARTEL PUBLICATIONS
PRESENTS

"Behold...
A new KING of street lit has arrived!"
-T. Styles, President & CEO, The Cartel Publications

ANOTHER NOVEL

HELL RAZOR Honeys 2 Furious

EYONE Williams

BEST SELLING AUTHOR OF FAST LANE & HELL RAZOR HONEYS

PUBLISHER'S NOTE:
This book is a work of fiction. Names, characters, businesses, Organizations, places, events and incidents are the product of the Author's imagination or are used fictionally. Any resemblance of Actual persons, living or dead, events, or locales are entirely coincidental.

Library of Congress Control Number: 2010928717
ISBN: 0982391358
ISBN 13: 978-0982391358
Cover Design: Davida Baldwin www.oddballdsgn.com
Editor: Advanced Editorial Services
Graphics: Davida Baldwin
www.thecartelpublications.com
First Edition

Printed in the United States of America

This book is dedicated to:
Everybody in the struggle everybody that has supported
me and everybody that knows what really goes on when
times get hard.

Eyone

Contact me at: eyone_williams@yahoo.com

What Up Superstars!

Well, Hell Razor Honeys 2 is finally here! And to think, HR1 dropped during the first year of business for the Cartel Publications. In fact, it was Hell Razor Honeys, Shyt List, Poison, Victoria's Secret and Pitbulls In A Skirt (which is soon to be a movie) that solidified our mark within the industry.

We were a baby pub back then but thanks to your desire for more, you've pushed us into the league with the big boys and as of today, we're 16 books strong and counting! We gotta love you for the support because it is through our talented authors and your word of mouth that any of this is possible.

And now, a couple of years later, Eyone is free from prison and already on the streets pushing his novel to new levels. He came hard with the first part of the series and did his job again with this one. You'll be on the edge of your seat as he whips you in and out of the streets of DC, New York and London!

So in regular Cartel Fan fashion, grab a seat, get your Snuggie, turn your phone off and let Eyone take you on an exciting mental journey of gigantic proportions!

Lastly, and as always, we want to pay respect to an author we love and appreciate for his/her literary journey or pen game. So it is with great pleasure that we pay homage to:

"*Leo Sullivan*"

Leo bogarted in the game with his thriller, *Life*, which happens to be one of my personal favorites. Since then he has given us, *Innocent* and *Dangerous* and we look forward to reading more from his highness.

Well, until I hug you later,

T. Styles
President & CEO, The Cartel Publications
www.thecartelpublications.com
www.facebook.com/authortstyles
http://www.ustream.tv/channel/tstyles/v3
http://www.youtube.com/user/tstyles74

Til Death Do Us Part

Murders had been committed, not one or two, but three. Three murders had been committed in a matter of moments. One of the murder victims was a D.C. Police officer. The shooting rampage took place on the mean streets of Southeast Washington, D.C. Now there was no turning back.

A speeding BMW wagon pulled into an apartment complex off of Silver Hill Road in Suitland, Maryland and parked in the back of the parking lot by the woods. Even in the darkness of night it was clear that the BMW had been involved in a gun battle. Bullet holes were all over the left side of the car. The back window was shot out. Smoke was coming from under the hood. The four occupants of the BMW were visually shaken-up and nervous. Behind the wheel of the BMW, Vida cut the car off, nervously looking around the parking lot. There were a few people outside and all eyes seemed to be on the BMW. Vida's heart was pounding rapidly, but she found some comfort in the fact that there were no police sirens in the air. Vida had done her job; she'd lost the police.

In the back seat of the BMW, Tia and Bloody, gripping Beretta machine guns, looked around nervously as well. They had sprayed bullets out of the back window of the car and flipped the first police car that gave the chase. The cop behind the wheel of the police car never had a chance when the .40 caliber slugs came crashing through his windshield.

Riding shotgun, Vida's husband, Moe-Moe, was shot. Through all the excitement and adrenaline rushing during the police chase, no one noticed that he was hit.

"Oh shit!" Vida shouted frantically, grabbing Tia and Bloody's attention.

"Moe-Moe!" Vida looked at the dark blood that covered Moe-Moe-s Prada shirt. He was bleeding from the left side of his stomach. "You're shot!!" Vida was on the verge of panicking. She quickly reached over and carefully pulled Moe-Moe's shirt up. Blood was gushing from his gunshot wound.

Tia and Bloody leaned forward from the back seat to see how bad Moe-Moe was hit. Tia sighed and shook her head, Bloody frowned at the sight of so much blood. They both knew Moe-Moe was hit badly. It looked like he'd been hit in the liver considering how dark the blood was.

"I'm okay." Moe-Moe grimaced. Beads of sweat covered his forehead. He'd taken a bullet as police fired on the BMW as it fled the scene of the murders around Atlantic Street. Moe-Moe didn't make a fuss about being shot because he didn't want to distract Vida as she tried to get them away from the police.

"Why the fuck you ain't say you was shot?!" Vida fought back tears. She was clearly emotional.

"Calm down, Vee." Moe-Moe pulled his shirt down.

Bloody cut in. "We gotta get you some help, Moe. You hit bad."

Tia nodded, "She right, we gotta get you to a hospital." Tia looked around the parking lot, anxious to keep moving.

"Fuck that." Moe-Moe said, sounding out of breath. "We gotta get the hell out of here. Police probably lookin' for us all over the place. We gotta keep movin'."

Vida closed her eyes, rubbed her head, and took a deep breath. She shook her head as she thought about the situation they were in. Shit was out of control and seemed to be getting worse by the second. Not only was the police after them in connection with three murders, but now her soul mate was shot and bleeding all over the place.

Vida's whole life had been turned upside down in a matter of an hour. His own cousin had kidnapped her husband for $500,000 and that led to the events that followed. Now, Moe-Moe was sitting next to her shot. Looking at Moe-Moe, Vida said, "We gotta get you to a fuckin' hospital. You're bleedin' too bad."

Moe-Moe grabbed Vida's arm firmly and said, "Vee, we just smashed two muhfuckas and a cop! If I show up at a hospital I might as well handcuff my-got-damn-self."

Tia sighed and shook her head. "He ain't gon' make it without a doctor."

Moe-Moe glanced around the car and said, "We need a new ride so we can get the hell outta here."

"Moe-Moe!" Vida shouted. "You not hearin' me, we gotta get you to a fuckin' hospital! We gotta get you some help!"

Moe-Moe closed his eyes, wincing in pain, and took a deep breath. "Vee, I'm not goin' to argue wit' you, we wastin' time." He put a hand over his gunshot wound and applied pressure in hopes of stopping some of the bleeding. Blood quickly covered his hand. Feeling short of breath, Moe-Moe looked back at Tia and said, "Get us a car, Tee."

Tia looked around and spotted a victim. "I got us." She said as she got out of the car with her Beretta machine gun behind her back.

Once Tia got out the car, Moe-Moe looked at Vida and said, "We gon' get me to a doctor as soon as we get out the area. Okay, Vee?"

Vida sighed. "Yeah, cool." Vida had her eyes on Tia. Moe-Moe took a shallow breath and began to feel dizzy. Vida noticed the look on his face and said, "Moe, you okay?!"

"Yeah... I'm... I'm..." Moe-Moe passed out and tumbled over onto Vida's lap.

"Oh shit! Moe-Moe!" Vida yelled.

Bloody sighed. What the fuck we gon' do now? She wondered.

"Oh my, God." Vida began breaking down. She had suffered too many loses— her mother, grandmother, and close friends/ family Tec and Ice. Vida couldn't stand to lose Moe-Moe.

"Is he breathin'?" Bloody asked with urgency.

"I don't know!" Vida yelled, lifting up Moe-Moe's head as she began to sob.

"Let me see." Bloody said. She got out of the car and opened Moe-Moe's door. "Turn him over, Vee." Bloody and Vida turned Moe-Moe on his back with his head still in Vida's lap. Bloody put her ear to his chest.

"Is he breathin'?" Vida blurted.

"Yeah." Bloody looked up at Vida. Bloody and Tia both had love for Moe-Moe, he was family. It hurt Bloody to see Moe-Moe in such bad shape; it hurt her even more to see the pain in Vida's eyes as she cried for her husband. Bloody wasn't used to seeing Vida in a position of vulnerability. She'd only known Vida for strength. "He still breathin', Vee, but we gotta get him to a hospital."

"Fuck!" Vida shouted through her sobs as she looked around for Tia. To be 24-years-old, Vida has been through too much in life.

Weakly, Moe-Moe sighed in pain as he opened his eyes and whispered, "Go 'head y'all... I... I... I ain't gon' make it..."

He was now covered with enough blood to be in a horror flick.

"I don't wanna hear that shit!" Vida shook her head. "You gon' make it. You gon' be fine! We ain't gon' leave you nowhere."

"I ain't gon' make it, Vee. I'm getting' cold." Moe-Moe said weakly.

"Come on, baby." Vida said through her sobs. "Hold on, just hold on. Tia went to get us a ride. We gon' get you to a hospital in no time."

Meanwhile, Tia was on top of business. She spotted a young dude sitting in a white Chevy Silverado pickup. Go-Go music was pumping out of the truck. The young dude that was sitting behind the wheel of the truck saw Tia's cute face as she walked his way. All he could do was flash a smile. Tia smiled back. This nigga sweet, she thought as she slid up on the driver's side window.

6

"What's up, ma?" the young dude said, looking like the Harlem rapper Jim Jones.

"You, sweetheart." Tia's smile vanished as she put the Beretta machine gun in the dude's face. "Get out the truck!" she hissed.

"Aight, ma." The dude looked like he was about to piss on himself as he raised his hands. "Don't shoot…don't do nothin' crazy. You can have the truck."

Tia snatched the door open and yanked the dude out by his LRG shirt. "Lay the fuck down and don't move!" Once the dude was face down on the ground, Tia pulled off.

Seconds later, Tia pulled up beside the BMW. "Come on y'all, get in!" Tia said out of the window.

Vida and Bloody helped Moe-Moe into the back seat of the pick-up. Vida sat with Moe-Moe while Bloody went to jump in the passenger seat. Tia hit the gas and took them flying out of the parking lot.

Cutting off the music, Tia looked at Vida through the rear view mirror and said, "What's the game plan, Vee? Where we gon' take 'em?"

Wiping tears from her eyes, Vida said. "The closest hospital we can find, Tee. Hurry up!"

Tia didn't even think about heading back into D.C. That was out of the question. She thought about Fort Washington Hospital. It was a good twenty minutes away, but it was their best shot.

As Tia pushed the Silverado along Suitland Parkway, Vida blocked everything out of her mind and focused only on asking God to pull Moe-Moe through. Wiping sweat from Moe-Moe's head as she slowly rocked him in her arms.

"You gon' make it, baby. You're strong...you gon' make it. You hear me?" Vida looked down into his eyes and said.

Weakly, Moe-Moe opened and closed his eyes trying to nod. He smiled. "I Love...You...Vee. I love...You...Baby."

Vida sobbed even harder causing her whole body to shake. Her tears fell upon Moe-Moe's face. "I love you too, baby. I love you so damn much." Vida leaned over and kissed his lips. "You mean the world to me." She whispered.

Moe-Moe nodded, struggling to breathe.

"No matter...No matter what happens...I want you to know..." He was seized by a violent coughing fit and began coughing up thick gobs of blood.

Vida began to panic. She didn't know what to do. Tia and Bloody took quick looks at the back of the truck to see what was up with Moe-Moe. They would never say it, but they knew Moe-Moe wasn't going to make it.

"Come on, Moe!" Vida sobbed. "Hold on, just hold on a little longer."

She pulled him tight into her chest and tried to hold onto him as if she could protect him from death.

"I... I..." Moe-Moe couldn't get his words out. "Love...Love...You, Vee."

"Don't talk, don't talk." Vida said with tears pouring from her eyes like a waterfall.

Moe-Moe took a deep breath.

"Vee, I love you." There was short exhaling after his words and then his body went limp in Vida's arms.

"Nooooooooo! Oh, God, nooooooo!" Vida screamed.

Sitting on the sofa in the living room of her boyfriend's apartment, Samara was still shaken up. Less than an hour ago Bloody was in the apartment with a Desert Eagle to Styles' head because Vida believed he had something to do with Moe-Moe being kidnapped. Samara had heard a number of stories about Bloody and was certain that Bloody would have killed her and Styles if Vida said so. Samara was beyond angry with Vida for sending Bloody to Styles' apartment with a gun.

In a murderous rage, Styles came out of the bedroom dressed in all black with a chrome Ruger .45 in his hand. He tucked the .45 in his waistband and grabbed his cell phone off the table. He had plans to knock Bloody's shit in the dirt, right along with Vida, Tia, and Moe-Moe since Vida was his wife. Styles flipped his cell phone open and called his man Eric.

"What's up, you ready, moe?" Eric answered the phone. Lil Wayne's flow could be heard in the background.

"Yeah, I'm waitin' on you, slim." Styles said as he grabbed an extra clip off the coffee table.

"See you in a minute, moe." Eric hung up.

Styles ended the call and put his cell phone in his pocket.

"What are you gonna do?" Samara looked up at Styles and said sounding worried.

"You already know the answer to that, Sam." Styles looked back at her and said.

"Bloody and them done crossed the line. They fuckin' wit' the right one now. They gotta answer for that shit!" Styles didn't hide his intentions from Samara. He trusted her.

"I know." Samara shook her head. She didn't like the situation. She and Vida had been friends since grade school. They'd been through their ups and downs, but Samara would never wish death on Vida or any of the other Hell Razor Honeys she came up with. But what could she say to Styles after Bloody came into his apartment and put a pistol to his head? There was no changing his mind.

"Styles," Samara said. "I don't want nothin' to happen to you, boo."

She knew exactly what Vida, Tia, and Bloody were capable of. She'd seen their work before and knew that they all got busy with that heat.

Styles walked over to Samara and rubbed his hand through her short and sexy hair. He kissed her forehead and said, "I'ma be just fine, Sam. You know that, baby girl. Don't worry 'bout me. I got this."

Samara nodded in agreement, although in her heart she didn't feel too good about what was about to come.

Styles' cell phone vibrated in his pocket. He pulled it out and flipped it open.

"Yeah, what's up, slim?"

"I'm out front, moe." Eric said.

10

"I'm on my way right now." Styles said.

He ended the call and looked at Samara.

"You gon' be okay here, or you want me to drop you off at home?"

Samara sighed. "I think I should go home." She got up and grabbed her Gucci bag.

Tia had pulled into a parking lot of an apartment complex off of Saint Barnabas Road in Temple Hills, Maryland and parked the Silverado in a dark corner under showing trees. Moe-Moe was dead. Everybody knew it, but Vida couldn't accept it. She was sitting in the back seat with Moe-Moe in her arms, sobbing her heart out. A huge piece of her died with Moe-Moe. Nothing would be the same ever again.

Bloody had taken a screwdriver she'd found in the truck and went to search for a car to steal, leaving Tia and Vida in the truck with Moe-Moe's bloody body. Looking back at Vida from the driver's seat, Tia wiped tears from her eyes.

"Vee, I know you hurtin' right now. I'm hurtin', too. You know Moe-Moe was family to me too, but we gotta go, Vee. We gotta leave him. He gone, Vee. If we don't get out of here now, we goin' to jail for life. You hear me, Vee?" Tia asked.

"We can't just leave him like this!" Vida yelled through her sobs. Her clothes were covered with Moe-Moe's blood.

"Look, Vee!" Tia snapped. "You emotional right now, but I ain't gon' let us go to jail! Fuck that! Now pull yourself together!"

Vida closed her eyes and clenched her jaw trying to block out the pain that she was feeling.

She couldn't stop sobbing, but she knew Tia was right. If they didn't keep moving they were sure to end up serving life in prison. Vida looked down at Moe-Moe's handsome face one last time. She kissed him softly on the lips, letting her tears fall freely. Memories of all the good times she and Moe-Moe had shared came back to her and made her sob even harder. She remembered how they first met and got together and their first kiss. The first time they made love. Their wedding, and honeymoon in the Virgin Islands. It has all been taken from her in one night.

A smoke-gray 2002 Dodge Viper SRT-10 with tinted windows pulled up beside the Silverado and the driver's side window came down.

"Come on y'all, let's go!" Bloody yelled.

Tia jumped out of the truck and opened the back door.

"Come on, Vee." She said sympathetically, placing a hand on Vida's shoulder. "We gotta go, boo."

Wiping tears from her eyes, Vida nodded at Tia.

"Okay." She slowly slid out of the truck, carefully laying Moe-Moe's head down on the back seat. She gave him one last kiss on the lips and said, "I love you. I'll always love you."

Stepping away from the truck, Vida shut the door and took a deep breath.

Vida and Tia climbed in the Viper. Bloody smashed the gas and took them flying out of the parking lot.

"Where we goin'?" Bloody asked looking at Tia who was riding shotgun. Bloody was also teary eyed behind Moe-Moe's death. It was a huge loss to their circle.

"Hit my stash spot out B-more." Tia said, rubbing her temples. She was still crying too.

"We can figure out our next move once we get there."

In the back seat with her arms folded, Vida was biting on her bottom lip as she tapped her foot repeatedly on the floor.

She couldn't stop crying. The only thing Vida could do was try and replace her sadness with anger. She felt like there was nothing else to lose. As she continued to cry a river hatred began to consume her and she could feel her heart growing cold.

B-More

Tia's Baltimore condo was perfect for a stash spot and a place to lay low. It was located in the heart of downtown and had a clear view of the harbor. Tia had it laid out as if she lived there. She didn't keep any money in that spot, only guns and drugs. Only Vida and Bloody knew where the spot was.

Tia, Vida and Bloody made it to the condo and got rid of their bloody clothes and the murder weapons. They took showers and threw on clothes that they had in Tia's closet. Their minds were racing in different directions. No one was sure what to do next. Bloody cut the TV on in the living room to see what was on the news. So far, nothing was on the news about their situation.

By now, Vida had cried herself out. She had no more tears. Anger was all she could feel. For the moment, anger felt better than pain.

While Vida was deep in thought, Tia and Bloody talked about what the next move was going to be or should be.

"I need some smoke." Bloody said. "My nerves still on edge."

Tia got up and headed for the bedroom.

"I got some haze, I'll be right back."

Waiting for Tia, Bloody looked at Vida who was sitting on the sofa watching TV in tight blue Gucci Jeans and a white Madness T-shirt. Vida's eyes were red and tired from all the crying. Bloody felt her pain, deeply. Vida was a sister to her. She hated the fact that there was nothing she could do to make her sister feel better.

"Vee," Bloody said hesitantly. "I'm really sorry 'bout everything... I really am."

"I know, B." Vida said never taking her eyes off the TV.

"Life's a bitch... a muhfuckin' bitch." She slightly shook her head in despair.

"It seem like everything I love in life is always taken from me. My mother, my grandmother, Tec, Ice, and now Moe-Moe. Sometimes I wonder what I've done to deserve this..." Vida shook her head again as her voice began to crack. Sadness covered her face.

"You and Tee are all I have left in the world. Don't nothin' else matter. Fuck it. I can't bring Moe-Moe back...you know?"

Bloody gave an understanding nod. "I feel you, Vee." She went over and sat beside Vida, rubbing her back. "I feel you."

"You know what I'm really fucked up about though?" Vida looked Bloody in the eyes.

"What's that?"

"We caught up in all this bullshit and we ain't even cause this shit It just came our way. I don't believe in luck but if I did I'd have to say our luck ain't shit."

Bloody shrugged.

"We gotta play the hand we dealt. Sometimes our hands be fucked up... but we gotta play' em. Shit, my hand been fucked up for as long as I can remember but I done had to play 'em. I feel your pain though, Vee." Bloody stated.

"I'm sittin' here wit' all kinds of shit runnin' through my mind right, and I'm thinkin' back to when Tec died... I use to ride around in the car by myself—I needed to be alone—and I would play that Tupac joint, *No More Pain*, over and over again. All damn day just wishin' that I would feel no more pain." Vida said as she rubbed her forehead, stressing.

"Now I understand that I can't get away from it. It's part of the life we live comin' from where we come from. We gotta deal wit' it."

Moments later Tia came back in the room with a sandwich bag full of purple haze and a sophisticated police scanner.

"Roll some of that shit. I need to put somethin' in the air bad." Tia said as she threw the weed to Bloody.

She then proceeded to hook up the police scanner. Baltimore police dispatching came over the airwaves but nothing was said about the girls' situation.

"You holdin' up, Vee?" Tia asked.

Vida nodded.

"I wish it was somethin' I could do." Tia walked over and sat on Vida's other side. She hugged her and kissed Vida on the cheek.

"It is what it is, Tee." Vida sighed and shook her head. "I don't even wanna think about it right now. It hurts too bad."

"I understand." Tia nodded. "We should be far enough from the city for right now." She continued glancing back at the TV.

Vida nodded. "I think so, too."

"Sooner or later they gon' connect us to that shit, though." Bloody said as she finished rolling the blunt of haze.

"You right. As soon as they find the BMW and Moe-Moe they gon' be lookin' for us." Vida said raising her eyebrows.

Lighting the blunt, Bloody took a long pull and held the strong smoke in her lungs.

"We need to get as far away from D.C. as we can. I ain't goin' back to jail, fuck that."

Tia sucked her teeth. "I ain't goin' back to jail either!" she stated firmly. "Not alive anyway. Feel me?"

Tia's cell phone vibrated on the coffee table. All three girls looked at it like it was a hissing snake for a moment. Vida picked it up and checked the caller ID.

"It's Samara." She said.

"See what's up wit' her." Tia said, getting the blunt from Bloody.

Vida answered the phone. "What's up, Sam?"

"Vee?!" Samara said excitedly.

"Yeah, it's me, Sam." Vida said flatly. She still had love for Samara, but wasn't in the mood to deal with her. She had to keep in mind that Samara was Styles' girl and Styles was now an enemy. Vida has her guards up.

"What the hell is goin' on, Vee? Tell me somethin'." Samara asked.

"Sam, I just lost my husband. I'm really not in the mood to talk right now. I do want you to know that I never meant for you to get caught up in this bullshit. You still family, Sam."

Samara could hear the pain and frustration in Vida's voice.

"Vee, they got you and Bloody all over the news…on every channel. The police is lookin' for you two for some murders…they say y'all killed a police and some other people-"

"Sam, I can't talk right now. I gotta go."

Vida ended the call and flipped the phone shut then looked at her partners in crime.

"They got us on the news in D.C., me and Bloody anyway." Vida said.

Tia looked confused. "Just you and Bloody?"

Vida nodded. "For right now." She told them what Samara said on the phone.

Shaking her head as her high began to set in, Bloody said, "The heat is on now."

"Yeah," Vida sighed. Looking at Tia. "Pass that smoke."

Tia passed the blunt to Vida. Vida took a long, hard pull and hit the blunt like it would be her last.

"We gon' need some cash to hit the road wit'." She managed to say while still holding the weed in her lungs.

"We can't risk goin' back into the city." Tia said while rolling another blunt.

"Yeah, I know." Vida said.

"All I know out here is coke and hammers." Tia said.

Bloody took a deep breath, she felt the walls closing in on them.

"Who can we get to bring us some cash?" Vida asked.

Before Tia could answer, her cell phone vibrated again. Vida grabbed it.

"It's Wendell." Vida said.

Wendell was the closest thing Tia had to a boyfriend.

"Let me see that." Tia said.

Vida tossed her the phone. Tia flipped it open and answered it.

"Yeah."

"What's up, Tee? You 'aight?" Wendell sounded extremely concerned.

"Not really." Tia sighed.

"What's up? I saw your girls on the news. What the fuck is goin' on?"

It's a long story. I'll tell you 'bout it later, but right now I need a big favor, Dell."

"What? Anything for you, Tee."

"I need some cash bad. Where you at?"

"My apartment." Wendell told her.

"Can you meet me in B-more, like right now?"

"Yeah, I can do that. How much cash you need?"

"'Bout fifty Gs."

"Say no more. Where you want me to meet you?"

"Meet me at that Egyptian Pizza joint I took you to last week."

"I'm on my way right now, Tee." Wendell ended the call.

Tia flipped the phone shut.

"We got some cash on the way." She said as she lit the blunt in her hand.

The sounds of a headboard banging against the wall, bed springs being worked overtime, and moans of a young female getting her full satisfaction filled the small Saratoga Avenue apartment in Northeast, D.C. Lil Rose had Paris' legs in the air, digging deep into her tight, wet pussy at a sweat-drenching pace. They were both rolling off "E" pills and purple haze. They showed no signs of slowing down anytime soon.

"Aaaahhhh…Yeah, Rose…" Paris' eyes rolled back in her head. She looked like a 21-year-old Amerie with a little more thickness in the hips and thighs. Paris was in an erotic trance. The "E" had her pleasure multiplied ten fold. Every orgasm she had thus far was like a nuclear explosion of sexual bliss. In her mind, Lil Rose was fucking her like she'd never been fucked before.

"Oh yesssss…ssssssssss… don't stop, Rose! Make me cum again, fuck me! Fuck me! Fuck me! Fuck this pussy…Aaaahhh!" Paris yelled.

Lil Rose's face was dripping with so much sweat that he had to close his eyes to stop it from getting in them. With every thrust into the tightness between Paris' legs Lil Rose let out a deep grunt. The pussy was on 1000 and climbing.

"Oh shit, that's my spot…that's my spot…oh my god! Don't stop, don't stop… ggggrrrrruuuhhhhaaaaaa.

Aaaaahhh." Paris began to shake. "I'm cummin', I'm cummin' again!" she shouted.

Moments later, Lil Rose exploded inside her, filling his condom.

"Damn, girl." He said as he slowed down stroking her creamy pussy long and deep, making her purr with satisfaction.

"You got that shit that make a nigga come home at night." He smiled.

"You fucked the shit out this pussy." Paris said trying to catch her breath.

Lil Rose smirked as he slid out of her and flopped onto his back.

"I gotta get in that shit one more time before the night is over." He looked at Paris and said.

"Hell-to-the-no, you beat the pussy up enough for one night." Paris got out of bed ass-naked and glistening with sweat. "I'ma hop in the shower real quick. I gotta meet Lala and Tera at the club. You know the Hell Razor Honeys gotta be in the spot deep." She threw her ass seductively as she headed for the shower.

"Y'all need to leave all that beefin' and shit alone." Lil Rose lit half a Dutch he had on the nightstand. "Yall look too good to be up in a club fightin' and cuttin' bitches."

"If bitches stay in they fuckin' place it wouldn't be no shit." Paris bent the corner and went down the hallway.

Lil Rose shook his head and smiled as he thought about how wild Paris and her crew was. They were the new age Hell Razor Honeys, the young girls picked up where Vida, Tia, Ice and the rest of the crew left off. Paris was a lot to handle. She was the unofficial matriarch of the Hell Razor Honeys, as far as the young girls were concerned that ran with her. Paris was also Samara's little cousin; she started running with the old Hell Razor Honeys right around the time Vida went to college. Paris paid her dues, although Samara always tried to stop Paris from running with the crew. As time went on the older girls in the crew grew out of hanging out and fighting bitches at the club but Paris found that the younger girls in the crew began to look at her like girls once looked at Vida and Tia. Although Samara was her older cousin and she admired Samara, Paris wanted to be like Vida and Tia, from afar. Nowadays, it was Paris that called the shots for the new Hell Razor Honeys and they were every bit of twenty deep now.

Lil Rose grew up on the same block with Vida, Tec and Samara. He really didn't get caught in the street life until he was about 15. He started selling coke for Tia around that time. From there he started getting a few dollars. He was loyal to the death and he loved Tia like a sister. He and Paris were tight as well but they weren't a couple. They were more like homies/fuck buddies. They both loved the arrangement just as it was and wouldn't have it any other way. Lil Rose blew weed smoke in the air, grabbed the remote off the nightstand and cut the TV on. As soon as he flicked to the news he saw Vida and Bloody. They were wanted in connection with the murder of a police officer.

"Damn, moe!" He turned the volume up to hear exactly what was being said. He grabbed his cell phone and called Tia.

Outside of the Egyptian Pizza joint in the stolen Viper, Tia and Bloody awaited Wendell's arrival. The night was quiet and windy.

A few people were out and about in this section of Baltimore. Nevertheless, Tia and Bloody were on high alert, strapped with .40 Caliber Rugers. Vida stayed behind at the condo. She needed time to herself to deal with Moe-Moe's death. Tia wanted Bloody to stay behind to keep an eye on Vida but Bloody insisted that she take the ride.

Looking at the Ruger lying across her lap, Bloody thought back to the first time she and Tia were on the run together. They'd left town for a minute and popped back up later to kill all witnesses to their murder. That got them cleared of all charges. The present situation was far more complex. Bloody glanced over at Tia.

"I wish we could clean this shit up like we did in that shit about Ice."

Tia shook her head, keeping an eye out for anything out of place.

"Shit different this time 'round. We smashed one of them boys in blue. They fuuuucked up 'bout that. They gon' be out for blood 'bout that shit there. The best thing we can do right now is get the fuck outta town." Tia stated. Bloody nodded.

"I feel you on that one, boo." Her eyes were barely open as she spoke; the haze had her nice.

Tia's cell phone vibrated in her pocket. She pulled it out and checked the number. It was Lil Rose. He was a little brother to Tia. She answered the phone.

"What's good, Rose?"

"What's up wit' you, Tee?" Lil Rose sounded concerned.

"It's a long story, boo."

"Aye, moe they got Vida and Bloody on the news and shit. On everything, kill."

"Yeah, I'm hip." Tia said.

"You okay, Tee?"

"I'm alive, so I'm cool for right now. I'll put you on point at another time. I'm on top of somethin' right now so let me get back at you. Keep your head up. You'll hear from me soon."

"Be safe, Tee. You know I'll kill a rock about you and put a brick in the hospital."

Tia laughed. "I love you, boy." She ended the call. As she put the phone back in her pocket she saw Wendell's Land Rover pulling up across the street.

"Keep your eyes open. I'll be right back." Tia said tapping Bloody on the leg.

She got out of the Viper and walked across the street in all black. Her Ruger was tucked in her waistband.

"What's up, boo?" Tia said as she climbed in the passenger's seat of the Land Rover. She leaned over and kissed Wendell on the lips.

"What the hell is goin' on, Tee?" Wendell looked across the street at the tinted window Viper.

Tia gave Wendell the quick version of the events that had her, Vida, and Bloody on the run.

"Damn, Tee." Wendell sighed.

"I feel you but I can't change it now. All I can do is get the fuck out of town."

"Where you goin'?" Wendell asked.

"I ain't sure yet. I'll get in touch wit' you in a few days."

Wendell shook his head and sighed. He couldn't believe that such a bad ass honey like Tia could be in so much drama. He had serious feelings for her and didn't want to see her hit the road.

"I'ma miss you, Tee."

Tia put both of her soft, small hands on Wendell's handsome face and pulled him close to her. She took a deep breath. She loved the African musk he wore. It turned her on. She kissed him deep and passionately for what seemed like hours. Their tongues caressed one another. As Tia broke their embrace she softly bit and pulled on his bottom lip.

"I'ma miss you, too. You my nigga." She winked at him.

"Call me if you need anything. At anytime. I got you. You hear me, Tee?"

"I will. Now let me get on the move, boo. Where that cash at?"

Wendell grabbed a brown paper bag from the back seat and handed Tia the bag.

"That's seventy-five Gs right there."

"Thanks, Dell." She gave him another kiss on the lips and got out the truck.

Wendell watched her walk back to the Viper. He was feeling her like no other but he had to let her go.

Back in the Viper, Tia sat the bag of money on the floor between her legs…almost under the seat and pulled out into traffic.

"We got seventy-five Gs." She said while glancing at Bloody.

"That'll hold us for a second. We'll find our way." Tia laughed.

"We always do. Don't we?" Bloody followed.

"You got that right."

Tia adjusted the rear view mirror looking back at Wendell's Land Rover. She would miss him.

A few blocks later, Tia looked in the rear view mirror again and noticed something.

"Them peoples just got on our back." She said.

Bloody looked over her shoulder and saw a Baltimore City police car behind them.

Her heart began to beat faster as she gripped her Ruger, trying to stay calm. She cut her eyes at Tia.

"Run them peoples, Tee. They can't fuck wit' you behind the wheel."

"Hold fast, they might not be fuckin' wit us."

"Fuck that, Tee, don't let 'em call back up. Step on them peoples." Bloody coached while looking over her shoulder again.

"Fuck it, you right." Tia stomped the gas pedal on the Viper throwing their bodies back in the seats as the car rocketed down the street, switching lanes, flying around cars. The lights on top of the cop car came on as the siren hit the air. The chase was on. Tia was giving the cop car the business, flying through intersections at top speed. A left here, a right there, but the cop car was keeping up.

"Shit!" Tia made a hard right swerving through on-coming traffic.

"Bus' a left! Bus' a left!" Bloody shouted looking over her shoulder.

"Hold on!" Tia yelled making another hard right damn near putting the car on two wheels. She cut off a Caprice making it smash into a passing Accord. The police car skidded around the crash, staying on the Viper.

"Watch out!" Bloody shouted.

Out of the blue, a Chrysler smashed into the side of the Viper. Tia lost control and slammed into a parked Volvo. The cop car was about two blocks away. Tia and Bloody were shaken up but the police sirens were closing in fast. They had to get it together and make a run for it.

"Come on, B!" Tia grabbed the bag of money, pulling her Ruger and jumping out of the car. Bloody jumped out too and the girls ran in different directions.

The cop car slammed on breaks. A short white officer jumped out firing shots.

"Freeze!" The cop yelled.

In a flash, several shots were returned in his direction, forcing him to take cover and scream for back up over the radio.

Cornered

Police sirens filled the air. A police helicopter was in the night sky shining a bright light down on the dark and narrow Baltimore alley. Police cars were speeding through the alleys shining bright lights into dark backyards, making dogs bark. Cops were also on foot, guns drawn and flashlights out. German Shepards had been turned loose. The police were closing in on their prey and they were out for blood. One of their own had been smoked, shot in the face five times with a .40 caliber.

Trapped inside a dark garage, out of breath, Bloody slid a fresh extended clip in her Ruger and cocked the gun. A loud echo filled the garage.

"These muhfuckas gon' have to kill me." She said to herself, peeping through the dirty window that faced the alley. Quickly, she ducked as a light was flashed through the window. "Shit!" she whispered, squatting next to the door.

Holding the Ruger between her legs, with both hands she cocked the hammer, ready for her last stand. The loud barking of a dog outside of the garage made her heart beat faster. She knew she was cornered.

"Fuck it," she continued to talk to herself. "I'm ready."

Outside of the garage, shining a flashlight through the window with his finger on the trigger of his gun, a police offer called out, "Over here, guys! I think we got something!" As the German Shepard barked and scratched at the garage door, five cops crowded around nervous, with their fingers on the trigger.

"Kick the door open." An officer said. With force, the officer kicked the door open and let the German Sheppard rush inside.

BOOM! BOOM! Bloody punished the dog with quick shots to the head. Spinning toward the cops she kept firing .40 caliber slugs. The cop with the flashlight got it all in the face. The rest of the cops spread out as they opened fire on Bloody. As bullets tore through her body, Bloody rushed out of the garage firing at the cops.

"Ahhhh!" she yelled, making the handgun sound like a machine gun as fire spit from the barrel lighting up the alley.

A bullet hit Bloody in the head and blew her brains across the alley. Her body hit the ground with a hard thud. The surviving cops emptied their clips in Bloody's direction making sure she was dead.

"Vida! Vida!" Tia shouted shaking Vida out of her sleep.

"Huh? What the fuck?!" Vida woke up rubbing her eyes as she came to her senses. Reality kicked her in the chest.

The TV was already on the news and Bloody's situation was the hot topic.

"They got Bloody, Vee!" Tia was excited and out of breath. She looked shaken up. Focusing on the news and shaking her head in disbelief, Vida said, "What happened?!"

Tia paced the floor with her pistol still in hand.

"The feds got on our back...we ran 'em and crashed. We had to bus' at they ass and run. I got away but Bloody got cornered. She musta shot it out wit' them peoples."

"This shit can't be goin down like this!" Vida said while standing up shaking her head.

On the TV, the anchorwoman was at the scene of the shooting where Bloody took her last stand. Cops and the reporters were everywhere. The dark alley was lit up by the lights of news crews and police cars. Yellow tape has the scene of the main action sectioned off.

"Baltimore City police have lost two of their own tonight when a high speed chase turned into a deadly gun battle. Two female suspects opened fire on officers. One is still at large and the other is now dead after killing two officers. The identity of the slain cop killer is not yet-"

Vida cut the TV off.

"I can't listen to no more of that shit." Vida sighed and walked to the window rubbing her hand through her hair like the world was coming to an end.

Tia took a seat on the bed and stared at the floor for a second as she clenched her jaw in frustration. I told Bloody to stay behind, she thought. Now Bloody was dead. Tia felt guilty about letting Bloody go with her to pick up the money from Wendell. Looking back at the situation, Tia barely got away. Once she and Bloody jumped out of the Viper bussin' at the police and ran in different directions, Tia headed in a dark alley and came out on the other side where she jacked a Nissan 350zx and made it back to the condo. As soon as she got back she saw the news and knew exactly what was up.

Trying to clear her mind, Vida said, "It's all or nothin', Tee."

"Yeah, I know…we ain't got nothin' to lose." Tia said nodding her head in agreement, still staring at the floor.

"Damn!" Vida hissed as she took a seat beside Tia. "First Moe-Moe, now Bloody. Fuck!" She slammed her fist down on the bed.

"We gotta get outta B-more. We can't just sit up in here and wait for the feds to find us." Tia said.

"We can't go back out tonight, the feds gon' be all over the place." Vida said.

"Don't nobody know 'bout this spot, we gotta lay low until at least tomorrow night or somethin'."

"Yeah, I think you right." Tia said nodding her head. Vida sighed not knowing what to do next.

Saratoga Avenue was in full swing even though it was past one in the morning. It looks like D.C.'s version of the hoods on HBO's hit show, *The Wire*. Coke, dope, water, Ecstasy, you name it and you could find it around the "Toga" anytime of the day. In front of his apartment building with a few of his homies, Lil Rose was on the grind serving pipe heads hand-to-hand. Sells were coming left and right.

Although Lil Rose was up to buying a brick of coke from Tia, he still got out on the block and went hand-to-hand as if he was only buying quarter-ounces. He loved the block and put it and his homies before everything else in life. However, at this time, with the heat on Tia and Vida, Lil Rose was thinking about finding a new connect.

Marky came out the building smoking a fat-ass Backwood stuffed with weed. He was dressed in a red and black LRG T-shirt, black LRG jeans and red and black Jordan's. His Lil Wayne style dreads were hanging down his back. He and Lil Rose were partners, they were close like brothers. Marky was a smooth dark-skinned 19 year old but at the same time had no problem with gunplay.

Marky spoke to all his homies, showing love and then pulled up on Lil Rose.

"Ay, moe, you see that shit 'bout Vida and them on the news?" He asked.

Lil Rose nodded.

"Yeah, moe, they went the hardest, kill my mutha, Moe!"

"Damn!" Marky was impressed with the work Vida and her crew had put in. He didn't think about the repercussions of their actions. Taking another pull on the Backwood, he passed it to Lil Rose.

"Ain't no turnin' back after you do some shit like that, moe." He said.

"No bullshit." Lil Rose hit the Backwood long and smooth as a pipehead walked up and asked for a twenty. He served the smoker and turned back to Marky.

"They crushed a police, moe. The feds gon' be all over they ass."

"It gotta be life or death for me to crush a police." Marky said shaking his head.

"Me too." Lil Rose said looking up and down the block as a few cars cruised by, one was blasting Young Jeezy.

A young dude named Driver walked up on Lil Rose and Marky.

"What's up wit' y'all, Moe?" Driver asked.

"Ain't too much." Lil Rose gave Driver dap. Marky gave Driver dap as well.

"What you up to?"

"I got Lala upstairs." Driver said rubbing his chin with a smile.

Lil Rose and Marky laughed at Driver. Shorty was fly as shit at 16. He had a nice rap game too, when it came to getting pussy. For him to have Lala waiting on him up in his apartment was a nice catch for Driver. Lala was one of the baddest young Hell Razor Honeys that ran with Paris. Lala didn't give the pussy away easily. A nigga had to have paper or serious pull game.

"How you pull that off wit Lala, Driver?" Lil Rose asked. Driver smiled.

"Come on, moe, you all in my business now."

Lil Rose and Marky laughed. Lil Rose nodded in agreement with what Driver said.

"My bad, moe, you right." Lil Rose passed the Backwood back to Marky.

"Driver, let me ask you this, if you got Lala upstairs, fuck is you doin' down here rappin' wit' us for?"

"I'm tryin' to get a few pills." Driver said, pulling a knot of 20s and 50s out of the pocket of his Red Monkey jeans.

Marky pulled out a plastic sandwich bag full of green "E" pills.

"How many you want, Moe?" Marky asked.

"Five. What you gon' charge me?"

"Gimme fifty." Marky said.

Marky gave Driver five pills at wholesale price. Giving Marky and Lil Rose a pound, Driver stepped off.

"Catch y'all later."

"I fucks wit' shorty tough." Lil Rose looked at Marky and said.

"Me too." Marky killed the Backwood and plucked it in the middle of Saratoga Avenue.

A car full of bad ass broads pulled up in front of Lil Rose and Marky. Lil Wayne was pumping out of the speakers.

"Aye, Marky!"

A cute girl called from the passenger's side window of the Audi. Marky took a good look at the girls and saw that they were a group of the Most Wanted Honies that came through the Toga to cop pills from him.

"I'll be right back." Marky said looking at Lil Rose.

Marky walked up on the car and took a good look inside. Five Most Wanted Honies were inside dressed to impress in Louie, Prada, Gucci, you name it.

"What's up, Summer?" Marky smiled. He had fucked Summer once and wanted another shot but they kept missing each other.

At 19 years old Summer was a dime piece. She looked like the singer Rihanna in the face but had the body of a video model.

"Let me get five of them pills." Summer licked her sexy lips and said.

Marky served her and got $90 in return.

"I see you wit' your peoples but when can we hang out again?" Marky asked. Summer smiled.

"I'ma call you tomorrow." She winked at him.

"Sounds good to me" Marky nodded and stepped away and the Audi pulled off.

"Aye, Moe," Lil Rose said as Marky came back his way. "That bitch Summer like that. Stop handcuffin' that ho."

Marky laughed.

"I ain't handcuffin' her. Shoot your shot, Moe. I only hit that once. I'm trying to put my bid in again."

"I feel you, Moe." Lil Rose said looking over his shoulder at a crap game that had just started in front of the building.

"Aye, Rose!" A voice called from the darkness of the side of the building. Lil Rose and Marky suspiciously looked toward the cut.

"Who the fuck is that, Moe?" Marky said.

Squinting his eyes, Lil Rose saw that it was his pipe head uncle, Mechanic.

Mechanic was one of those cool-ass smokers that would bring a nigga a thousand sells and only want a twenty for it. He was always selling something, fixing something, or renting his car out to get high.

"Come here, shorty, I got somethin' for you." Mechanic said waving his hand urgently for Lil Rose to come holla at him.

Lil Rose tapped Marky on the arm and said, "I'll be right back." He then stepped off.

"What's up, Unc?" Lil Rose said in the shadows on the side of the building with Mechanic.

Mechanic had a book bag in his hand.

"Check this out," he opened the book bag and pulled out a beat up Uzi machine gun, the small pistol kind. The clip had to be a foot and a half long.

"This one of them nine millimeter Uzis, here...check it out." He handed Lil Rose the Uzi.

Lil Rose admired the machine gun with both hands, turning it from side to side. The joint looked wicked.

"Man, do this joint work?"

Mechanic sighed.

"Come on, family. You know better than that." Mechanic said. Lil Rose smiled.

"What do you want for it?"

"Two hundred."

"This joint better work." Lil Rose said unsure.

"Trust me, it work, shorty." Mechanic stuck his hand in the book bag and pulled out a silencer for the Uzi.

"I got this too."

"Damn, moe." Lil Rose was excited. He pulled out the money and gave it to his uncle.

"Catch you later, nephew." Mechanic stepped off.

Lil Rose walked up on the crap game with the book bag on his back and told Marky to meet him inside the building.

Once inside, Lil Rose said, "You ain't gon' believe what I've got."

"What?" Marky asked.

Lil Rose opened the book bag to show Marky the machine gun.

"We got a muhfuckin' U-whop."

"Damn, moe! And you got a silencer, too?!"

Lil Rose nodded.

"You tryin' to see what's up wit' them Panamanian niggas 'round the corner?"

"Kill." Marky nodded in agreement.

The next morning, Tia was packing a light bag of clothes and a few other things to hit the road with. She and Vida still weren't sure what they were going to do, but they knew they had to get out of the area. Bloody's last stand was still all over the news. Her real name was just released and she was connected to the D.C. murders. The whole story was now put together. Baltimore City police knew all about Bloody, Tia and Vida. Their names and pictures were plastered on all the news networks. Even CNN was in on the story now.

Finished packing a few things, Tia zipped the bag and took a deep breath. Stress was at an all-time high. The loss of Moe-Moe and Bloody was really getting to her. She could feel the walls closing in on her and Vida. At this point, Tia's mind was made up, it was kill or be killed, by any means. Just as Bloody had held court in the streets, Tia vowed to do the same if she and Vida were to find themselves cornered.

Walking over to the mirror in the bedroom, the one that hung on the closet door, Tia studied her new look. She'd cut her hair off and was rocking the short Halle Berry look. It fit her well, too, adding to her sexiness. She also popped in a pair of hazel contacts to help give her a different look. Picking up her .40 caliber off the dresser, Tia popped in a fresh clip and cocked the gun.

Vida walked in the bedroom in a pair of tight, black Seven jeans, a white Prada short sleeve shirt, and a pair of black and white Prada tennis shoes. She'd gotten Tia to cut her hair into a short bob and dyed it blonde like the Philly rapper, Eve. The look fit her well.

"Tee, I think we should head up north first." Vida said, checking out her new look in the mirror over the dresser. She looked very different. "Hit a busy place like New York until we figure out what to do."

"Yeah, I'm wit' that." Tia said as she picked up a Backwood stuffed with purple haze and lit it.

"I was thinkin' the same thing. We can holla at Tonio up there." Tia continued.

"Daddieo's brother?" Vida raised her eyebrow.

"Yea, slim got major connections, Vee." Tia took a long pull on the Backwood. "I'm sure he'll look out for us."

Tia and Tonio still did a little business together on and off since they were both heavy in the drug game.

Thinking about Tonio, Vida nodded her head and said, "Yeah, Tonio might be just the man to holla at."

"I got his number in my phone." Tia passed Vida the Backwood. "I don't wanna use that joint no more though, so I'ma have to call slim from a pay phone once we hit the road."

Blowing smoke in the air, Vida said, "Cool, we can do that." She took a few more pulls on the Backwood and passed it back to Tia. She needed the high that was coming on. Thoughts of Moe-Moe and Bloody were weighing heavy on her mind, stressing her out.

"Ay, Tee, we need a ride. We don't need to be in no stolen ride right now."

"I'm hip." Tia took a long pull on the Backwood.

"I'ma text Lil Rose and get slim to bring us one of his joints, he'll do that for us."

"Yeah, do that, Tee."

"Aye, Vee, I know you already know this but we can't go to jail. That's out of the question."

Vida nodded and sighed.

"I know. They can't take us alive... no matter what."

"We all we got now, Vee."

"Til' death do us part." "Vida hugged Tia.

"Til' death do us part." Tia held Vida tight.

Cali

On the West Coast, No Draws sat on the bed in her tiny cell dressed in a dingy orange, over-sized jail jump suit with her hair in a ponytail. She was reading the *Los Angeles Times* paper. Her present situation stayed in the news in one way or another. This morning the article painted a picture of her as an ambitious young woman who would do anything to succeed- even if it meant committing murder.

No Draws sighed and slammed the newspaper on the floor, frustrated. Since the murder of her business partner, Liz Whitaker, No Draws' life had become a living hell. Everything she'd worked so hard for was being taken away from her. There was a strong chance that she could face the death penalty if found guilty of Liz's murder. At this point in her life she was damn near alone and at her lowest point. The only person she could really count on was Daddieo. She loved him. Nevertheless, No Draws was holding on, she was tough; the D.C. streets had made her that way and she would never lie down without a fight. She had one of the best legal teams money could buy.

Thinking about her situation, No Draws began to pace the cell wondering what the government really had against her. Yeah, it was true that No Draws was behind the arsenic and nitroglycerin that was found in Liz's system, but who could prove it?

A short while later a C.O. came to No Draws' cell and told her that she had a legal visit waiting for her. Quickly, she got her legal papers together and was off to see her lawyer.

Inside a small, secluded conference room, No Draws sat down at a table across from her lawyer, Lawrence L. Stevens.

Lawrence L. Stevens was a handsome brown-skinned man a few months away from 35 years old. He had the look of a young Denzel Washington. He and No Draws were friends; they met a few years back through Malcolm-Jamal Warner. Lawrence was one of the best and highest paid, black lawyers in Hollywood. He was all the hope No Draws had.

With her hands folded on the table, No Draws flashed a weak smile and said, "Anything new?" She desperately needed some good news.

Flipping through some legal papers, Lawrence removed his Gucci glasses, sat them on the table carefully and said, "Michelle, I'm working hard, I have my investigator turning over every stone, but right now I have nothing new to tell you."

No Draws sighed.

"Lawrence, I'm payin' you top dollar. I need you to make this shit go away." She paused and leaned forward for emphasis. "The government has nothin' on me but hearsay…all bullshit. You can eat that shit up."

"And I will." Lawrence said in his smooth voice, placing his hand on No Draws'.

No Draws felt comforted by his touch and the sincere look in his brown eyes.

"Let me do what I do best, Shelly." He rubbed her hand softly. "I know all of this is hard for you, but trust me. I will clear your name and get you out. Okay?" Lawrence raised his left eyebrow in a sexy, authoritative way.

No Draws nodded, trusting Lawrence. "Okay," she said as she rubbed his hand, playing with his wedding ring.

Smoothly pulling his hand away, Lawrence opened one of the folders he had on the table.

He looked over a few notes and said, "Shelly, what can you tell me about Marky Miles the Third?"

The name instantly rang bells for No Draws. Marky Miles III was an influential black movie producer in Hollywood. No Draws had blackmailed Marky out of the leading female role in a John Singleton movie, and a million dollars to start her own production company. Her blackmail tool was a tape of Marky in a hotel room bent over with ten inches of hard dick in his ass.

Thinking about Marky, No Draws nodded her head and said, "Marky's an undercover meat lover."

"A what?" Lawrence looked confused.

No Draws smiled, clearly amused. "He's a fag, and I blackmailed him wit' that information. Why, what made you ask about him?"

"He's one of the witnesses against you." Lawrence flipped through some more papers. "The DA thinks Mario can help put the whole case-"

"Bullshit!" No Draws snapped. "He can't do nothin' but lie on me!" Her cute face began to turn red.

Lawrence reached out and placed his hand on top of No Draws' to comfort her.

"Calm down, Shelly. I got everything under control. I just needed to know that."

Pissed off, No Draws said, "I'm goin to ruin his ass! Watch! He fuckin' wit' the right one."

"Shelly, don't do anything rash, not at this time anyway. Promise me that."

No Draws sighed. "Okay." In her mind she was already putting together her plan to ruin Mario.

After going over a few more things with No Draws, Lawrence told her that he'd see her in a day or two. Holding her hand, he said, "I'm going to get you out of this mess, trust me."

"Okay." She nodded.

Back in her cell, No Draws thought about Mario and smiled. I guess he think he can get me back by working with the DA, she thought. I got a trick for his ass though. Lying back on her bunk, No Draws tried to clear her mind. Her fate was up in the air.

Under the star-filled sky a dark-blue Mercury Grand Marquis made its way up I-95 with Lil Wayne's, "Go DJ", pumping through the speakers. Vida was gazing out of the passenger side window with a chrome 10m Ruger lying across her lap. Thoughts of Moe-Moe and Bloody would give her mind no rest. Shit just didn't seem real. Tia was behind the wheel with a Mac-10 on her lap, by no means was she playing games. Any cop trying to take her into custody was in for the fight of his life.

With $75,000, a few outfits, a pair of fake IDs, and some ammo, Vida and Tia put the D.C. area behind them forever. Nothing about their future was certain.

"Aye, Tee." Vida said out of the blue.

"Yeah."

"You think we could get out of the country?" Vida continued to gaze out of the window.

Tia sort of shrugged and said, "I'm sure we could, but not wit' these IDs we got right now. We'd have to get fake passports and some more shit."

"Yeah, I was thinking the same thing." Vida looked at Tia.

"I'm sure we can get fake passports and all that shit in New York."

"Fuck yea, money can buy a muhfucka anything in New York. We just gotta find the right peoples, you know how that go." Tia glanced in the rear view mirror and saw a Pennsylvania state trooper about five cars back. She tensed up a little bit, even though the car they were in belonged to Lil Rose and was legit.

"Aye, Vee, state troopers a few cars behind us." Tia said calmly.

Vida's heartbeat sped up. She didn't look back though.

"How many cars behind us, Tee?"

"Bout five." Tia's hands began to grow sweaty as flashbacks of the police chase in Baltimore came to mind.

"Play it cool, Tee." Vida gripped the 10mm as she took a look back at the state trooper.

Suddenly the state trooper's lights came on and the sirens blared. The car sped up, passing two cars in the far left lane of the highway.

"Don't jump the gun, Tee." Vida's heart was now pounding as if she was trapped on a crashing plane.

The state trooper swerved over two lanes to the right, one car behind the Grand Marquis.

Tia's eyes darted from the road to the rearview mirror, back and forth. It was taking every ounce of self-control she had not to stomp on the gas.

The state trooper swerved back into the far left lane and flew up the highway after a black corvette. The girls breathed a sigh of relief.

Cutting her eyes at Vida, Tia said, "I was ready to haul ass, Vee, no bullshit!"

Shaking her head, Vida sighed and said, "I feel you." Her heart was still pounding.

The Toga

It was business as usual around Saratoga Avenue. Young dudes had the block on lock, grindin'. Junkies were chasing their next high. Music was pumping out of the passing cars. A police car cruised through the block here and there but the action never stopped. Tonight, the Hell Razor Honeys were on the scene. Paris, Lala, and Tera were all on the grind pumpin' "E" pills. They had all the sells. Back to back, cars were pulling up looking for "E" and one of the three Hell Razor Honeys would make the sell. The girls were safe around the Toga. No one would fuck with them in the hood that they called home. The older Hell Razor Honeys had already paved the way for them.

Paris, Tera, and Lala were the backbone of the new era Hell Razor Honeys. They were the wildest three and the only three that were truly from Saratoga Avenue. When it came to beefin' they were the quickest to slice a motherfucker as well. They really weren't into gunplay like Vida, Tia and Ice had been. However, Paris had shot at a few bitches before. In one way or another, the new era Hell Razor Honeys had run-ins with a number of girl crews in the city, namely, *Most Wanted, Fuck'em Up, KO, Pussy Pound, X-Rated* and a few others.

But nowadays, Hell Razor and Fuck 'Em Up Honeys were cool.

Paris was the 21-year-old, hot headed so called leader of the Hell Razor Honeys who looked like the singer Amerie. Paris carried the Hell Razor Honeys torch with pride and would slice a bitch in the blink of an eye if they disrespected anything or anybody that had anything to do with the Hell Razor Honeys.

Lala was the laid back, fly girl of the crew that all the niggas were chasing. At 19 years old she was already a pro at working the power of the pussy. Every nigga that had the honor of getting a taste of her swore that her pussy was on 1000. Lala somewhat looked like the Miami rapper, *Trina*. She would slice a bitch but she had to be pushed. However, once she was pushed she was as mean as a pit viper snake.

Tera at 21 years old, was a sexy, chocolate, stallion. She had no cut cards about sex. She liked to fuck. She didn't see herself as a freak or a roller; she saw the niggas she fucked as such. It was all about a nut with her. With her long silky black hair, slanty eyes and long eyelashes, Tera had that Foxy Brown look. She was also a natural hustler. Her only flaw, amongst the crew was that she was a shit starter. But, she could back it up.

Counting a handful of money after serving a car load of young dude's "E" pills, Tera looked at Paris and Lala and said, "I'm out, them joints went fast as shit."

Paris smiled. "Damn, bitch, let me find out you be sellin' your pills half price or somethin'."

Tera laughed. "Bitch, please! I need all mines. You know how I go about this ink."

Lala closed her cell phone and said, "Okay, ma I'ma start callin' you Rayful Edmonds. You gettin' all the sells."

Paris laughed.

Tera laughed, too, but said, "Don't call me no Rayful Edmonds, bitch, that nigga be snitchin'. I ain't wit' that hot-ass shit."

Lala laughed. "My bad, my bad, I ain't mean it like that, but you do be gettin' paper."

Paris said, "Yeah, no bullshit T, you be movin' them pills fast as shit." Paris' cell phone came to life with Lil Wayne's "Go DJ." She checked the caller ID and disregarded the call.

"We might as well re-up tonight." Looking at Lala, Paris said, "How much you got on you right now?"

"A little over five-hundred." Lala said.

"What about you?" Paris asked Tera.

"Seven-fifty." Tera said as she watched a red BMW 745 cruise down Saratoga Avenue.

"Ain't that them Panamanian niggas?" Lala asked.

"Yeah, thats them niggas." Paris said "Anyway, let me get y'all money and I'ma go re-up before we hit the go-go."

Lala and Tera gave Paris their money. Across the street where most of the dudes were, a broad by the name of Bria came out of the building with an attitude about something. She was cursing everybody out that looked at her.

Tera looked across the street and said, "Ain't that one of them *Most Wanted* bitches?"

"Yeah," Paris said. "That's the bitch Bria. Marky be fuckin' her. He probably fucked her and put her ass out."

Paris and her crew died laughing.

Walking across the street to her car, Bria saw the Hell Razor Honeys laughing and the Remy in her system had her feeling bold.

"Fuck is you bitches laughin' at?" Bria yelled.

"What you say, bitch?" Tera got dead serious.

"You heard what the fuck I said." Bria shot back.

Bad move on Bria's part.

Tera, Paris and Lala began walking in her direction.

Everybody outside knew it was about to go down and all eyes were on the Hell Razor Honeys.

"Dumb-ass bitch, I'ma beat your muhfuckin' ass!" Tera hissed.

Paris and Lala were closing in.

Face to face with Bria, Tera could tell the girl had been drinking.

"Your drunk-ass better watch your mouth."

Looking at the three girls that had her surrounded, Bria said, "You bitches ain't like that!"

Paris sucked her teeth and said, "Fuck all this talking!" She set shit off and blasted Bria in the eye with a crashing right hand that made Bria see stars.

"Ahhh!" Bria yelled out in pain as she began swinging punches. She refused to cower.

Like wild dogs, Paris, Tera, and Lala were all over Bria. Heavy punches and kicks rained down on every part of Bria's body that was exposed. Once Bria was on the ground the Hell Razor Honeys had no mercy. They put feet on her ass like she'd stolen from them.

Kicking Bria in the face, Paris shouted, "Dumb-ass bitch! Don't- be- comin'- 'round- here- talkin'- that- bull-shit!"

A few dudes rushed over to break up the slaughter. Bria's cute face was a bloody mess but she still kept running her mouth as niggas pulled Paris, Tera, and Lala off her ass.

Struggling to break free from her homie, Driver, Paris shouted, "Let me go, Driver, that bitch still runnin' her fuckin' mouth!"

Being helped to her car, Bria managed to say, "This shit ain't over."

"Bitch, fuck you! I'ma put that razor on your ass next time I catch your rollin' ass!" Lala shouted.

Inside a Montana Avenue apartment with two of his men, Warren sat on the run-down sofa counting money as a Backwood hung from his lips. Strong weed smoke floated up in the air making him squint his right eye. Warren was getting plenty of money around Montana Avenue with his coke prices. After his man Lito brought him to D.C. from New York and got him to run the Montana Avenue spot there was no looking back.

Flame, Warren's cousin, was in the kitchen at the stove cooking bricks. Three bricks were already rocked up, one was in the pot and one brick of powder was on standby. A chrome .45 was in clear view tucked in between Flame's waistband.

Jr. sat in a chair across from Warren playing with a .40 Ruger talking about the Hell Razor Honeys and how he wanted to fuck the one they called Paris. He'd been trying to get her for the last few weeks but Paris wouldn't give him or Warren any play because they were Panamanians.

In a thick West Indian accent, Warren said, "The girls act like they pussy made of gold."

Jr. laughed. "It might be."

"Fuck them yanky bitches." Flame yelled from the kitchen in his West Indian/ New York accent. "Them bitches gon' set your raas up for these niggas around here, you better keep your eye on this money."

Warren and Jr. gave each other a funny look and laughed at Flame.

Jr.'s cell phone vibrated in his pocket. He pulled it out and answered it. "Yea, what's the deal, Lito?"

Lito was the top man in their circle. Smoothly, Lito said, "How shit look on that end?"

"It's all good here. I'm 'bout to come through. Shit sweet." Jr. said.

"See you then." Lito ended the call.

Putting his phone back in his pocket, Jr. got up and grabbed a shopping bag with $50,000 inside. Looking at Warren as he headed for the door, putting the .40 in his waistband, Jr. said, "I'll be back, I'ma drop this money off over Lito's house."

"Okay," Warren nodded, still counting money.

Jr. left the apartment. Warren looked in the kitchen and said, "You finished cooking that shit yet?"

"I got one more to go." Flame said.

Warren walked in the kitchen and watched Flame work his magic at the stove. They began talking about the art of cooking powder to rock. Flame was a monster at the stove.

Moments later the front door eased open. The sound of keys made Warren look over his shoulder. He saw Jr. being led into the apartment at gunpoint by a dude in a ski mask.

"Oh shit!" Warren shouted, grabbing Flame's attention.

Flame spun around just in time to see Jr.'s brains get blown out by one of two masked gunmen. Flame went for his pistol. "Fuck!" he shouted.

The second gunman opened fire using an Uzi with a silencer on it, spraying bullets all over the apartment in one deadly wave. Bullets tore through Flame before he even got a hand on his pistol.

Filled with bullets, Warren and Flame fell to the floor, slumped in sick positions. Quickly, the gunman with the Glock slid up on the bodies and put two slugs in each head without the blink of an eye. He then looked at his partner with the smoking Uzi and said, "Let's clean this muthafucka out, moe."

On The Run

A light rain fell outside as Vida looked out of the window of a New Jersey motel that she and Tia checked into with Tia's fake ID. They were right outside of New York so there would be no problem hooking up with Tonio.

Looking over her shoulder at Tia who was sleeping like a baby, Vida sighed and shook her head as she thought about their situation. Stressed out, she lit the Backwood full of weed and took a long pull as she turned her gaze back out the window. Her mind was consumed with all the shit she and Tia were now caught up in. Ain't no looking back now, she thought as she blew a grayish cloud of smoke into the air. The future looked dark and hopeless, but Vida knew she had to deal with whatever came her way at this point. Thoughts of her grandmother came to mind as she continued puffing on the Backwood. She shook her head as she thought about how she'd promised her grandmother that she would change her life for the better. In reality, Vida had changed her life for the better but when Moe-Moe was kidnapped she had no control of the drama that followed. "Damn," Vida whispered to herself. "I'm sorry, Grandma."

"Who you talkin' to, Vee?" Tia said in a groggy voice as she wiped sleep out of her eyes.

"Huh?" Vida turned to face Tia.

"Who was you talkin' to?" Tia sat up, yawning and stretching.

Vida shrugged. "I was just thinkin' out loud, I guess." Vida walked over and sat on the bed beside Tia.

"What you thinkin' out loud about?"

"All this bullshit that we done got into."

Vida hit the Backwood long and smooth, holding the smoke in her lungs she passed the Backwood to Tia.

Tia hit it and closed her eyes as she held the strong smoke in her lungs.

"Vee, shit is what it is. We can't trip off of what we can't control." Vida looked at Tia with a smirk on her face and shook her head. "What?" Tia blew smoke in the air.

"You wild as shit, Tee."

"Vee, I'm just lookin' at this shit for what it's worth. We in too deep, boo… it's all or nothin'."

Vida nodded in agreement. "Yeah, you right."

Tia passed Vida the Backwood.

Vida took a quick pull and said. "Fuck it." She was high as shit now, feeling at ease. "We might as well try to hook up wit' Tonio today and get out of this cheap-ass motel."

Standing up, stretching again, Tia said, "Sounds like a plan to me."

"I hope Tonio can help us, Tee."

"You know main man got pull, I know he can help us." Tia walked over to the TV and cut it on. On BET they were talking about the news of Lil Kim going to prison. Tia turned to the local news, nothing there caught her attention. However, when she turned to CNN her heart skipped a beat and she got a sick feeling in her stomach. Pictures of Vida and Tia were on the screen, the story was about how they were wanted for the murder of police officers in Baltimore and D.C. Tia cut the TV off.

"Why you do that?" Vida asked.

"We don't need to hear that shit. We know all we need to know, they on our ass."

Vida sighed and shook her head. "At least we look a little different right now."

"Yeah, that should get us by for a minute in New York, it's millions of faces all over the city."

Tia headed for the bathroom. "I'ma take a shower real quick, when I get out I'ma call Tonio from the pay phone."

"Bet," Vida laid back on the bed, stressed out. Fuck it, she told herself. She thought about Tonio for a second and wondered if she and Tia could really trust him to help them out. Thinking about Tonio made Vida think about her ex-boyfriend Daddieo. Daddieo and Vida could never be cool again, not after Daddieo started fucking with No Draws. After a little thought Vida told herself that Tonio was the best shot she and Tia had if they were going to survive on the run.

Twenty minutes later, Tia was on a pay phone with Tonio. The pay phone was a few doors down from the motel the girls were staying in. While Vida kept an eye out for anything out of place, Tia explained to Tonio that she needed to hook up with him because she needed his help. Tonio had seen Vida and Tia on CNN but he still told Tia that she could meet him at his store in Harlem.

Tia looked at Vida and winked. Addressing Tonio, she said, "We'll be there in a little while, Tonio." She hung up the phone and tuned to Vida. "Let's hit the city."

In the back office of, Uptown Gear, in Harlem, Tonio's urban clothing store, Tonio shook his head as he shut his phone and slipped it in the pocket of his Gucci jeans. He was amazed that Vida and Tia were in so much shit. He respected the girls and had love for them. If there were any way he could help them he would do it.

Lighting a fat-ass Dutch full of haze, Tonio took a seat on the soft, black leather sofa that sat against the back wall and grabbed the remote. He cut on the 60" plasma TV that hung from the wall of the plush office. He put the TV on ESPN and kicked his feet up on the coffee table as he enjoyed the haze.

A knock on the door grabbed his attention. "Yeah, come in." Tonio shouted.

Tonio's man, Born, came in the office and shut the door behind him. Born was sort of an enforcer for Tonio. Since Born wasn't good at getting money in the drug game, Tonio paid him to collect money and put heads to bed if niggas got out of line. Born was good at that and had been good at that since his teenage years. He looked a lot like the Philly rapper, Beanie Sigel.

"What's up, son?" Tonio said. He could tell that something was on Born's mind. "What's on your mind?"

"If it ain't one thing, it's another," Born said shaking his head and taking a seat in the black leather chair to the right of Tonio. "Son we got a problem…" he rubbed his chin. "Word on the streets is a nigga got a hit out on you, kid."

Tonio remained calm and blew smoke in the air. It wasn't the first time he'd learned that someone wanted him dead.

"You know who got the hit on me?" Tonio leaned over and passed Born the Dutch.

"I'm on it, but I'm not sure who put it out yet." Born took a long pull on the Dutch and held the smoke as he spoke.

Tonio nodded, understandingly. He wondered who had the hit on him. He was getting tons of money and knew for a fact that haters were around every corner.

"You know who took the hit?" He asked Born.

"I ain't sure, but my man in Brooklyn on top of that for me right now."

Born blew smoke in the air and passed the Dutch back to Tonio.

"I'ma have a name real soon and I'ma put a bullet between his eyes."

Tonio smirked. "That's why I fuck wit' you, son. You 'bout your business." He took a pull on the Dutch. "How you come across this info?"

Born smiled, watching ESPN. "You pay me to come across info like this, right?"

"No doubt."

"I got a man that take hits, he put me up on game, but didn't have no names at the time. You know how the streets work."

Tonio nodded.

"I'm by your side everywhere you go until I get to the bottom of this bullshit."

Nodding his head in agreement, Tonio said, "Cool." Standing up, Tonio walked to his desk and opened the top drawer. He pulled out a small Uzi pistol. The machine gun had a 25-shot clip. Checking the long clip, Tonio said, "It's too hot outside to be ridin' around in a vest so we gon' have to keep our eyes open. I don't wanna play no games."

"Say no more, son." Born lifted up his Gucci T-shirt and flashed his lightweight bulletproof vest. "But all that about not wearin' no vest, I ain't feelin' that."

"Yeah, I know, I know." Tonio pulled out his cell phone and made a quick call. Once he was done with the call he said. "I gotta meet Romel a little later to holla at the connect. I don't think-"

Born cut Tonio off. "Nah, son, I'm goin' everywhere wit' you. Fuck that. I don't even wanna hear it."

Tonio smiled and nodded his head. Born was loyal. "I respect that."

"Good."

"I got company on the way over here in a few. After that we gon' slide to the spot and collect that money."

"Cool." Born said. "Who's the company?"

"You saw them D.C. girls on the news this mornin'?" Tonio raised an eyebrow.

"The ones that killed them jakes?"

"Yeah." Tonio sat on the desk. "They need my help."

"Ain't that Daddieo's old girl?"

"Yeah. I got a lotta love for them girls. They wild as shit though. You were locked up when I was dealin' wit' them for real, but you'd love them." Tonio smiled and shook his head as he thought about how wild the Hell Razor Honeys were. "Son, when I say wild, I mean they will smoke a muthfucka. I ain't seen no broads like them in a long time."

"You sure they ain't gon' bring us too much heat… shit, they got the feds on they heels." Born said with a concerned look on his face.

"I thought about that, but fuck it, they need me so I'ma look out as best I can." Tonio shrugged.

A knock on the office door cut into the conversation.

"Yeah, what's up?" Tonio yelled.

The door cracked and a pretty brown skinned girl stuck her head in the office.

"Tonio, you got two girls out here lookin' for you."

"Send 'em in, Niya." Tonio nodded.

Niya disappeared and pulled the door shut.

Looking at Born, Tonio said, "That's them right there. Let me holla at them alone for a second."

Born stood up. "I'll be right outside the door." As Born left the office he passed Vida and Tia. He spoke and couldn't take his eyes off of them. Tia really caught his attention.

Tonio smiled as Vida and Tia stepped inside his office and shut the door behind them. He hadn't seen them in a good while. Their new looks fit them well.

"Damn, you two look good as shit." Tonio walked over and gave Tia and Vida hugs. Although he knew they were on the run, and that had to be stressful for them, he could tell that there was more to Vida's stress by the cold look in her eyes.

"Have a seat." He motioned toward the sofa.

Vida and Tia took a seat.

"Want somethin' to drink?" Tonio asked.

"Nah." Tia said.

Vida declined shaking her head.

Tonio took a seat in the chair to their right and said, "Well, tell me what's up. What the hell is goin' on wit' y'all?"

Tia explained everything to Tonio, keeping it gangsta. Vida sat back and let Tia do all the talking. Tonio shook his head when Tia told him how Moe-Moe's cousin was behind all the bullshit that had her and Vida on the run.

Still shaking his head, Tonio said, "That's some foul shit."

Tia agreed. "Yeah, I'm hip. So here we are." She cut her eyes at Vida.

Now Tonio understood why Vida seemed so cold, she'd just lost her husband.

"I'm sorry to hear 'bout your husband, Vida, I really am. I know how it is to lose somebody that close."

Tonio paused for a second as he thought about how his old girlfriend had been kidnapped for $500,000. He paid the money and the dirty motherfuckers still murdered his girl. Pushing the painful thoughts out of his head, Tonio looked up at Tia and Vida and said, "I'm here for you. Whatever you need."

"First of all, we need somewhere safe to lay low, and some new IDs. The ones we got are Baltimore joints. I don't want shit to connect us to D.C. or Baltimore." Tia said.

"I feel you," Tonio rubbed his chin. "I can get right on top of that, that ain't shit. I'll get y'all some New York IDs by tomorrow."

Vida finally spoke up. "Tonio, you think you could get us some passports?"

Tia gave Vida a sideways glance; she knew what Vida was thinking about.

Tonio smiled, nodding his head. "I like that, Vida. You thinkin' big."

"It's no lookin' back," Vida shrugged. "They got us all over the news and shit. We can only run for so long."

Tia nodded. "No bullshit."

"I gotta check around wit' a few people, but money will get anything you want. I'm sure we can get two passports, no problem at—."

Tonio's words were cut short by the thunderous sounds of gunfire outside of the office door. The gunfire made Tonio, Vida, and Tia jump. They all went for their guns instinctively.

CARTEL PUBLICATIONS PRESENTS

Back in Maryland

50 Cent's hit song, *In Da Club* was pumping through the powerful stereo speakers in Styles' living room. Weed smoke filled the air as he and his young protégé, Eric, sat on the sofa playing Madden '05 on Play Station. Styles worked the Dallas Cowboys while Eric was working the Washington Redskins. The Redskins were up 21 to 10 over the Cowboys. Styles and Eric were chillin' now that they'd learned about what was up with Vida and her crew. After looking for Vida and her crew without success, Styles and Eric called it a night and crashed at Styles' Silver Spring, MD condo. When they woke up Vida and her crew was all over the 12:00 news, again. The feds had raided the homes of Vida, Tia and Bloody. $700,000 in cash, guns and drugs were confiscated. *The Washington Post* was calling Vida and Tia "Queen Pins" that ran a violent gang of girls called the Hell Razor Honeys.

Styles' cell phone came to life with the sounds of Young Jeezy's "Soul Survivor" and Styles paused the video game. "Hold fast, shorty." He took the call. It was his man, Eyes. Eyes was supposed to introduce Styles to a new cocaine connect. After a few words, Styles ended the call and resumed the football game.

"That was Eyes, he 'sposed to put me down wit' that Panamanian connect he got. Shit should fall in place after that, feel me?"

Eric nodded, blowing weed smoke in the air.

"Hell yeah, Eyes and Creek gettin' that paper fuckin' wit' that Panamanian connect. You gon' be right back in the pocket fuckin' wit' that nigga there. On everything, kill, moe."

Styles nodded thinking about the possibilities of being back on his feet in the drug game.

"We'll see how it go down. I hope it all works out, 'cause if it don't I'ma be on my strong arm shit again."

Eric laughed. "That's right, moe, get on your Wayne Perry shit."

Styles laughed as he hit the Backwood.

"I wish I woulda knew that bitch Tia was movin' all that work, I woulda been on my Wayne Perry shit but I thought Moe-Moe was callin' the shots for real."

"I don't know why you thought that, Tia and them had they hands in a rack of shit for the longest. Everybody knows that, moe." Eric threw another touchdown on Madden.

Styles threw the controller down on the sofa.

"You got that game, joe. I got too much shit on my mind." Styles killed the last of the Backwood and dropped the roach in an empty bottle of Remy that sat on the table beside the sofa. He looked at his iced out Gucci watch and saw that it was 1:43pm.

"I gotta make a few runs before I slide around the park to meet Eyes."

"I might as well ride wit' you. I gotta take my mother some money anyway." Eric cut off the Play Station and the TV. "I'm 'sposed to pick up Paris later on."

Styles looked at Eric and smiled. "You still fuckin' wit' Paris?"

"Yeah, fuck that nigga Lil Rose. She ain't his bitch." Eric said, checking the clip in his Ruger.

Since Lil Rose and Eric were both fucking Paris they had bumped heads over her a few times, but neither one of them left her alone. Paris' pussy was too good. However, it was Eric that carried the hard feelings over Paris.

Styles shrugged. "You better leave Paris alone before you catch a body over her fast ass."

"Come on, moe. I ain't gon' in like that over no bitch."

"If you say so." Styles smiled as he headed for the door.

"I don't know nothin' 'bout no murders!" Samara shouted, feeling pressured by the two FBI agents that were standing in the living room of her apartment questioning her.

With the murders of law enforcement, the feds were bringing down the heat. They were pressing everybody that had a connection with Vida, Tia or Bloody. Being as though Samara was close to the girls, the agents decided to pay her a visit and see what they could squeeze out of her. They asked her countless questions concerning the murder and drug dealing, but what they seemed the most interested in was what led to the shootings that left the D.C. police officer, Moe-Moe and two others dead.

Giving Samara a stern look, a Steve Harvey looking agent by the name of Brewer made a statement.

"Get this clear, since you want to act like you don't know anything, your friends have been under investigation for over two years. We know all about them and the gang you all started, the Hell Razor Honeys. We know that you know more than you are telling us."

Agent Arnold, a short white man with blond hair and blue eyes, cut in.

"Young lady, Agent Brewer is being nice. I'm going to be a little more straightforward. We're going to make your sweet little life a living hell if you don't give us-"

Samara snapped. "I don't know shit got dam it! What the fuck you want me to do?"

Brewer and Arnold gave each other quick glances. They knew they were getting under Samara's skin. With a little more pressure, they were sure they could break her.

Agent Brewer smiled a little and said, "You're a smart young lady, don't go down for something your friends did. We're giving you a chance to help yourself now. In a minute we're going to start making arrests and everybody that's close to your friends are going away for life."

The thought of going to prison for life shook Samara, she couldn't act as if it didn't.

"I told you I don't know shit!" She folded her arms pissed off. "As a matter of fact, it's time for you muh-fuckas to get out...I don't have to listen to this shit. I ain't did shit!"

With a nod, Agent Brewer said, "Have it your way. We'll be seeing you sooner than later."

Agent Arnold gave Samara a wink. Both agents headed for the door.

"I know my rights!" Samara yelled as the agents left the apartment.

Even after the agents were gone Samara was still nervous and jumpy. She wondered if they could really put her with all the shit Vida and Tia were caught up in. Without a second thought, Samara grabbed her phone and called her lawyer.

With a chome 9mm in his waistband as he walked down the small hallway of the Montana Avenue apartment building, Marky tensed up with apprehension when he saw the two FBI agents coming out of Samara's apartment. Marky could spot feds from a mile away. His dreads hung over his face so they really couldn't get a good look at him as he passed them.

What the fuck the feds doing coming out of Samara's joint, Marky thought as he headed down the hall to Tera's apartment without looking back at the feds. Thoughts of the murders he and Lil Rose put down crossed his mind for a second. They had murdered all three Panamanians in the robbery and came off with five bricks of coke and $65,000 in cash. Homicide detectives had come and gone more than once since last night's slaughter.

Fuck it, Marky thought as he knocked on Tera's door, watching the feds bend the corner.

Moments later, Tera opened the door wearing nothing but a long gray Prada T-shirt, looking good as shit.

"I thought you was comin' over last night, boy." Tera said.

With a distracted look on his face, Marky stepped inside the apartment and shut the door behind him. "I got caught up."

Walking to the kitchen throwing her sexy ass, Tera said, "What's on your mind, you look like you just lost some major paper or somethin'?"

Marky smiled, looking around the clean, laid out apartment that Tera lived in by herself.

"Nah, I ain't lost no paper. I just saw the feds comin' out of Sam's apartment." He flopped down on Tera's cream-colored sofa and grabbed the remote. He cut the TV on and went straight to BET. Mike Jones, Slim Thug, and Paul Wall were on the screen "Still Tippin'".

"What's that all about?" She yelled from the kitchen.

"Man, I don't even know." Marky said although he really wanted to know what the feds were talking to Samara about. With all the dirt that he and Lil Rose done around the way, he didn't feel comfortable with the feds talking to folks that knew him. An idea popped in his head.

"Aye, Tera, why don't you call her and ask her what that shit was all about. Act like you seen the feds comin' out her spot."

Coming into the living room with a huge glass of orange juice, Tera said, "Look, I thought you came over here to get up in this pussy. Now you got me on all kinda moves." She took a seat beside Marky and grabbed the phone off the coffee table.

Marky smiled and rubbed a hand through her hair.

"That's why I fucks wit' you."

Tera reached Samara, she made small talk and then got to the point. Samara told Tera why the feds had been to see her. A few moments later Tera ended the call and told Marky what was up.

With an arm around Tera, Marky said, "Damn, the feds pressin' her 'bout Vida and them, huh?"

"Yeah, you know how that shit go." Tera sat the glass of orange juice on the table. "Shit hot as a muhfucka 'round here. You know them Panamanian niggas up the street got smoked last night, three of 'em." She continued.

"Yeah, I heard 'bout that shit there. It was on the news this mornin'. I saw homicide up there a little while ago. Fuck that shit though, them bammas shouldna' been 'round here no way." Marky said with a straight face.

With a sexy smile on her face, Tera said, "My pussy was wet all night thinkin' 'bout you, nigga."

"I can't tell."

"What you mean by that?" Tera rolled her eyes, playing with Marky's long dreads they reminded her of Lil Wayne.

"I heard you and your partners in crime beat the shit outta one of them Most Wanted bitches."

With a playful attitude, Tera said, "Yeah, we beat the shit outta that rollin' ass bitch, Bria you be fuckin'."

Marky smirked.

"Yeah, I know you be fuckin' her rollin'ass."

Marky laughed and tried to brush the conversation off. He and Tera were only fuck buddies so they could talk about things like Marky fuckin' Bria.

"So now y'all gon' be beefin' wit' Most Wanted?"

"Them bitches don't want no problems wit' us, you know Hell Razor run the city."

Marky laughed.

"Fuck all that, I ain't thinkin' 'bout them Most Wanted bitches." Tera unzipped his blue Gucci jeans. "You know what I'm thinkin' 'bout." She got on her knees and pulled out his manhood. Looking him in the eyes, she stroked him up and down with her soft, small hands. The red polish on her nails was to Marky's liking. "I been thinkin' 'bout this big dick all night." She put her tongue out and took one long, wet lick from the base of his dick to the tip, it made the whole thing wet. He grew hard like magic, right in her hand.

Marky smiled, rubbed his hand through her silky hair, and said, "Show me how much you was thinkin' 'bout me." Looking down into her pretty eyes as she continued to lick his erection, Marky removed his pistol and sat it beside him on the sofa. Her tongue was sending chills through his body with every long lick. From root to tip she put him in her mouth with passion, over and over. Her head went up and down with Superhead skill. Marky watched and was turned on by the sight of his dick vanishing in and out of Tera's mouth.

Coming up off his dick for a second, Tera licked her pretty lips and said, "You like it?"

Marky smiled. "Yeah, fuck yeah. Don't stop." He pulled her head down on his dick and watched her go back to work. Vicious!

She sucked him off some more and then decided to tease him a little bit. Just as Marky began to moan she pulled him out of her mouth with a popping sound. "Is it good?"

She rubbed his wet dick all over her cute face as if she loved it. She licked it, kissed it and then put it back in her hungry mouth. Tera's mouth made wet, greedy sounds as her head bounced up and down. She was in her zone, sucking the life out of him. Her hair rubbed against his leg, it sent tingles up his spine. Marky used his free hand to play with one of Tera's hard nipples. Her head skills made him moan. He began to pull her head down further on his dick making her deep throat him. Tera used one hand to caress his balls smoothly. Sucking and stroking with her other hand, she pulled Marky closer to his orgasm. He held his nut back with all he had; the head was too good to let it end so fast.

Tera looked into Marky's eyes as she went up and down on his dick. She knew she was driving him crazy by the way he was thrusting up into her mouth, hitting the back of her throat. "Mmmmmmmmmhhhmmm." She encouraged him to fuck her mouth.

Marky's cell phone went off with sounds of Lil Wayne's "Go DJ". His eyes darted to the caller ID. It was Lil Rose's ringtone so he really didn't have to look at the number. Looking from the phone back to Tera, he locked eyes with her as she continued to suck the life out of him. She looked so good with him in her mouth. Her eyes begged him not to take the call, but he had to, Lil Rose was his right-hand man.

"What's good, moe?" Marky said sounding preoccupied with ecstasy.

"Where you at?" "Lil Rose said. Sounds of being on the block filled the background.

Pissed off that he answered the phone, Tera put her all into her oral magic.

Marky's eyes rolled back in his head. He bit down on his bottom lip.

"I'm… ahh… I'm over Tera's joint."

Lil Rose laughed. He understood what was going on.

"When you finish what you doin' come through here. I need to put you on point 'bout somethin'."

"Bet." Marky ended the call and tossed the phone to the side. Putting both hands behind Tera's head, he began to fuck her mouth like a pussy. Her moans let him know that she loved it. "This what you want?" He said as he pumped in and out of her mouth. She welcomed his mouth fucking and deep throated him with ease. He moaned as his testicles tightened and he knew he was about to nut.

"Ahh… I'm 'bout to cum." He continued to fuck her mouth. His hips rose off the sofa as he tried to get deeper into her mouth and down her throat. He closed his eyes and moaned like it was the best head in the world. "I'm 'bout to cum…. Ahh…" He was seconds away and couldn't hold it any longer. Tera couldn't wait. Then boom! Like a shotgun, he came hard and strong in her satisfying mouth. Tera's eyes grew big as she enjoyed his explosion and swallowed his innermost juices like it was sweet nectar.

"Ahhhhh… damn." Marky looked down and watched as Tera sucked out the last of his load.

Licking her lips, as a little cum dripped down her chin, Tera said, "I been waitin' all night for that."

Marky smiled, still rubbing her hair. "You get your fill?"

She kissed his dying erection, licked it, and said, "You gotta fuck me before you leave nigga, it ain't goin' down like that."

Marky laughed. "I ain't got no problem wit' that. You know I gets down for mine."

Tera stood up and stretched. "Let's take it to the bedroom.

"Don't meet me there, beat me there." Marky told her as he grabbed his pistol and followed Tera to her bedroom.

'Round The Way

Movin' and groovin', Saratoga Avenue was in full swing. Even though the feds had been through the hood, nothing changed. The show went on, niggas had to eat so they were on the grind. Lil Rose was front and center, pumpin' coke from the Panamanian robbery. He was so numb to the streets that he was a part of, that the murders he and Marky had committed didn't even bother him. All he was concerned about was getting paid. However, when he saw the Panamanian, Lito, riding through the hood asking questions, Lil Rose felt that he and Marky may have a situation on their hands since the Panamanians they robbed and slumped were Lito's peoples. Fuck it, Lil Rose thought, he and Marky would deal with it when and if they had to.

Across the street from where Lil Rose and the other young dudes were, Paris and Lala were standing outside of Paris' Honda Civic pissed off and sweating in the hot ass sun. They were on their way to the mall but Paris' car was acting up so they had to get pipe head, Mechanic to take a look at it.

With her arms folded tapping her foot impatiently on the cracked sidewalk, Paris sucked her teeth and said, "It's too damn hot out this bitch."

Watching a white Range Rover come down Saratoga, Lala said, "We need to go back inside until he fix the car... a bitch gon' need a shower standing out here in this damn heat." Lala looked down at her sexy body. She was killin' 'em in her skin-tight Gucci shorts. Her sexy legs were glowing in the sun.

Raising his head up from under the hood of the Civic, Mechanic said, "I'll have your ride ready in a minute, Paris. Don't even trip, baby girl."

Paris walked over and took a look under the hood.

"What the hell is wrong wit' my car? Why it keep actin' up?"

"Bad alternator. I can get you a new one, you already know that."

"For how much?"

"Gimme a hundred right now and I'll snatch you one before the day is over."

Paris dug into the pockets of her Prada jean skirt and pulled out a thick knot of big bills and peeled off a fresh one hundred dollar bill.

"Here you go." She handed Mechanic the money. "Let me hold your car for a few hours."

Stuffing the money inside the pocket of his dirty jeans, Mechanic said, "Driver got my car right now, but don't worry, your shit is gon' hold up until later on. I got you covered, baby girl."

"Mechanic, don't have me all the way out Rockville and my shit won't start." Paris said firmly.

While Paris and Mechanic spoke about the car Lala had pulled out her cell phone to text Driver and digitally flirt with him, letting him know that she couldn't wait to see him again so he could tear the pussy up. The young nigga put in work and Lala couldn't get him off her mind.

Moments later, Driver hit back: "I ain't trying to be cocky, but I knew you would be feeling me. I told you, next time will be better!"

Lala smiled, but her smile quickly faded when she saw a white Audi bend the corner, heading her way. The car was packed with at least five Most Wanted Honies, as far as Lala could tell. She could mark out Bria riding shotgun, Summer behind the wheel and at least three other girls in the back seat. Closing her phone, ready for whatever, Lala called out, "Aye, Paris, we got action."

"What?" Paris looked around and saw the Audi coming their way. "Fuck them bitches thinkin' 'bout comin' 'round here?" She quickly pulled out her Dolce and Gabbana earrings.

Mechanic looked up sensing danger.

The Audi pulled up and stopped right in the middle of Saratoga Avenue. Bria, Summer, and three other Most Wanted Honies jumped out in T-shirts, sweats and tennis shoes, ready for work.

Summer glared at Paris and said, "Bitch, you gotta fuckin' problem?!"

Paris shot Summer a look that said Bitch, you got me fucked up!

"Fuck all that talkin' what you bitches wanna do?" Paris raised her arms like, What's up?

Bria snapped. "Fake ass bitch!" She rushed Paris, but was caught with three swift blows before she was able to get a hand on Paris' hair. The two girls got busy like pit bulls in a small cage. Summer rushed in to help Bria, punching Paris in the back of the head as she grabbed her shirt. Lala charged Summer, pulling her hair and pounding her in the face. Wasting no time, the other three Most Wanted Honies joined the drama. In no time, it was a gangsta girls party. Most Wanted was giving Paris and Lala the business, although the two Hell Razor Honeys were standing firm, fighting back like there lives depended on it. Amazed that the girls were in the middle of the street like a scene out of the movie, *Gangs of New York*, Mechanic tried to break up the huge fight. Lil Rose and a few of his men ran over to help break up the fight as well. Lil Rose didn't like the fact Most Wanted was getting out on Paris and Lala.

As the girls were pulled apart, punching, kicking, cursing, and clawing, Paris and Summer had each other's hair and wouldn't let go. They wouldn't stop swinging either. As Lil Rose struggled to pull the two girls apart, Paris was steady going off, trying to tear Summer's ass up.

"Let me go Rose! I'ma kill this bitch!" Paris shouted, snatching out a patch of Summer's hair as Lil Rose got her up in the air kicking and screaming. "Put me down, Rose! Let me at that bitch!"

Police sirens hit the air close by. The girls were still trying to kill each other.

Lala, with a busted lip, shouted, "You bitches done fucked up now!" Mechanic held Lala back. "Five of you dirty ass bitches can't even fuck wit' us!"

Struggling to get loose from the grips of one of Lil Rose's men, Bria spit on Lala and shouted, "Fuck you bitch, you Hell Razor bitches ain't shit!"

Two police cars with flashing lights and blaring sirens came flying down the street. With no questions asked, everybody took off running when the law hit the scene. The police cars stopped in the middle of the street and four officers jumped out going after the Most Wanted Honies as they all jumped in the Audi. But the Most Wanted Honies were too fast. Once inside the Audi, Summer stomped the gas and hauled ass down Saratoga Avenue.

It only took Paris and Lala a hot second to run through the cut and hit the back door of Lala's apartment building. With swift steps they ran up the steps and were inside Lala's living room in no time. Catching their breath as they looked out the window to see what the police were doing, Paris and Lala looked at each other without saying a word for a second. They knew each other so well they knew what was on each other's mind.

Paris, out of breath still, said, "Them bitches gon' get everything they lookin' for now, fuck that!"

Putting a hand to her busted lip, Lala tasted blood. "I'm cuttin' them bitches up when we catch'em."

Paris was pissed off to the point of thinking about murder, even though she wasn't a killer. She hated the fact that Most Wanted had gotten the best of her and Lala. In no time the streets would be talking about how Most Wanted got out on Hell Razor. Paris hated that thought. She had to set shit straight, no matter what the cost.

"We gon' get everybody together and run them bitches down right now. Fuck later!"

Lala's house phone rang. Paris grabbed it, it was Tera calling, she'd already heard what just went down.

"We gon' punish them bitches!" Paris stated with anger and conviction. "Meet us down here."

"I'm on my way right now." Tera hung up the phone.

Marky met Lil Rose inside the Saratoga Avenue apartment building that they hustled in front of right after the drama between Most Wanted and Hell Razor. After Lil Rose put Marky on point about the girls he got to the important matter.

Standing at the end of the second floor hallway with Marky, Lil Rose said, "Aye, moe, I saw the Panamanian dude, Lito, ridin' around talkin' to a few people. I'm sure he was askin' about that move we went on."

In a hushed tone, Marky said, "Who was he talkin' to?"

"A few smokers...a few bitches." Lil Rose said as he watched two pipe heads go inside an apartment at the other end of the hall.

Marky rubbed his chin for a second as he thought about Lito. He knew Lito was the top man who first opened the Montana Avenue spot.

"Don't nobody know we smoked them Panamanians." Marky shrugged, he didn't give a fuck about Lito asking questions. "You wanna smoke the nigga Lito? He can get it too."

Lil Rose smiled. "I fucks wit' you, moe. You 'bout that work."

"I ain't got no problem puttin' that hot shit in Lito's ass. For real for real, we shoulda been ran them niggas from 'round here."

Lil Rose nodded. "I don't know, we gon' lay back for a minute. If the nigga keep comin' back 'round here askin' questions we gon' give his ass the business."

"That's right." Marky gave Lil Rose some dap. "I dare his ass to set up shop 'round here again."

Moving on, Lil Rose said, "We should be good for a second now we got them bricks, but we still gon' have to find a new connect."

"Yeah, I'm hip, but we shouldn't have no problem findin' no connects as long as our paper is right and our paper gon' be right as soon as we get rid of this shit we workin' wit' now."

"No doubt," Lil Rose pulled his vibrating cell phone out of his pocket and looked at the number. It was one of his freak bitches. He'd get back to her later.

"Look though, I'ma holla at my cousin up Kennedy Street and see if I can get us a nice connect. I'll let you know something later on."

"Bet."

"Let's hit the block and get this money then." Lil Rose said. He and Marky headed down the hall.

Stepping out of the building, Lil Rose and Marky were attacked by the heat. The block was back in business like the police had never been on the scene minutes ago. Rap music was blasting out of a blue Impala SS that was now parked in front of the building. Driver and his little crew of 15 and 16 year olds were sitting inside the car drinking Remy.

Lil Rose nodded toward the Impala with a smile and said, "That Lil nigga Driver wild as shit, moe."

"No bullshit. We need to put shorty on the team. He way before his time and he thorough, too." Marky said looking up and down the block.

"You think shorty can move some weight?" Lil Rose asked.

"Hell yeah. Why?"

In a hushed tone Lil Rose said, "We can put some of that work in his hands and it won't look like we done got our hands on a rack of coke overnight. Feel me?"

Marky nodded with an approving smile. "That make a lot of sense."

"Why don't you pull up on shorty and see where his mind at?" Lil Rose suggested.

"I'm on it right now, now." Marky stepped off to holla at Driver.

"Aye, Driver, let me holla at you, Lil moe."

Lil Rose made a few sells while Marky was talking to Driver.

Moments later, a silver Lexus GS 430 pulled up and parked behind Driver's Impala. The chrome 22-inch rims on the Lexus were gleaming in the sun. Even with the smoke gray tinted windows all the way up, The Game's, "Hate It or Love It", could be heard loud and clear. Lil Rose looked at the Lexus suspiciously even though he knew it was Styles' car. However, Styles only came around there to see Samara and Samara lived a block over on Montana Avenue, so what business did he have on Saratoga Lil Rose thought?

The passenger side window of the Lexus came down slowly.

"Aye, Rose," Styles called out. "Let me holla at you real quick, slim!"

"What's up, moe?" Lil Rose said as he approached the car. Leaning inside the passenger's side window. "What's good?"

Styles leaned over towards Lil Rose and said, "Who got them "E" pills?"

Nodding towards Marky, who was standing outside the driver's side of Driver's car, Lil Rose said, "My man, Marky, got them joints."

"I'm tryin' to get a few, tell shorty let me holla at him." Styles said, turning the volume down on his powerful stereo system.

"Aye, Marky!" Lil Rose waved Marky over to the Lexus.

Marky walked up on the driver's side of the Lexus. Styles gave Marky a pound.

"Let me get five of them "E" pills." Styles pulled a thick knot of bills out of his pocket and handed Marky $100 bill.

Marky took the money and pulled a plastic bag of "E" pills out of his pocket. Looking up and down the street with a quick glance, Marky smoothly handed Styles the pills.

"Good lookin' homes." Styles said. As he looked down into his hand he felt something slam into the front of his car with extreme force.

"Man, what the fuck?!" He shouted, pissed off.

Driver had accidentally backed his Impala into Styles' Lexus.

Styles jumped out of his car, heated.

"What he fuck is wrong wit' your dumb ass?" he shouted at Driver as he looked at the damage to the front of his Lexus.

Marky had a wild look on his face like he wanted to laugh.

Lil Rose could feel the tension. He just shook his head and wondered how the situation was going to play out.

"Damn, moe!" Driver stepped out of his Impala high as shit. "My bad."

Enraged, Styles looked at Driver and shouted, "Your bad?! Fuck you mean, your bad?!"

Seeing where shit was going, Marky stepped between Styles and Driver.

"Hold up, Styles. Shorty ain't mean to back into your shit."

Lil Rose stepped into the street between Styles and Driver as well.

Driver frowned up his face and said, "Moe, you can kill all that loud talkin' you doin', I ain't tryin' to hear that shit. You got me fucked up!"

"Got you fucked up?!" Styles tried to rush Driver but Marky held him back.

"Hold up, Styles!" Marky said.

Lil Rose tried to hold him back as well.

"Don't take it there, Styles. I'll pay for it."

In a flash Driver pulled an AK-47 assault rifle out of his car.

"Let that nigga go!" he shouted, holding the choppa with both hands. Driver's four young homies stepped out of the car with big boy shit that had extended clips hanging to the ground.

Styles saw the firepower Driver and his crew was working with and came to his senses real quick!

Looking at Driver and his crew, Lil Rose said, "Hold fast! Lay back! Lay back!"

Driver glared at Styles and responded to Lil Rose, "You tell that nigga to lay back talkin' all that bullshit." Driver was pressing the issue now.

Styles was thinking about living to fight another day.

"Shorty, you got it." Styles put his hands up like, I don't want no trouble."

Driver said, "yeah, aight."

Lil Rose shook his head. He knew the situation was out of control but it was no way he could change it at this point.

"Aye, Styles, I'll pay for your shit, moe."

Styles shook his head as he jumped back in his car.

"Don't even worry 'bout it, shorty." He pulled off without another word.

Lil Rose and Marky looked at Driver and his crew who were still in the street holding their guns. Lil Rose and Marky shook their heads.

With a sigh, Marky looked at Driver and said, "Shorty, you dead wrong. You know better than to whip out on a nigga and don't bus'."

Lil Rose agreed with a nod. "It's gon' be some shit now."

"You shoulda let me smoke the nigga then." Driver said as his crew got back in the car.

Lil Rose sighed.

"You might be right, but it's too late for that right now."

Driver got in his car. "Fuck that nigga!"

Uptown Shoot Out

Gunfire tore through Uptown Gear. People inside the store were screaming and running for cover. Some were running out the front door while bullets flew in all directions. Two masked gunmen had stormed inside the store with automatic handguns and opened fire on Born. About his business, Born dove behind the metal counter in the far right corner of the store and let loose on the two gunmen. With his Glock .40, Born let off careful shots at his attackers. The gunmen were serious about their work. They were duckin' behind everything that could provide cover but still gunning for Born, all in seconds.

The door to the back office flew open and Tonio, Vida and Tia came out bussin' like a scene out of the movie, *Dead Presidents*. Surprised, the gunmen adjusted quickly. They were outnumbered with bullets flying by their heads so they tried to make a move for the door.

Vida and the taller of the two gunmen crossed paths and traded shots. The gunman tried to fire from behind the CD rack. Vida seemed to be on a death wish, not taking cover, just blasting with a distant glare on her face. The gunman popped out and fired three shots at Vida. They all flew past her head. She could actually hear the slugs whiz by her ear. Without a blink of an eye she put two slugs in the gunman's chest with her 10mm. He stumbled backwards with his arms flinging in the air wildly. Vida was dead on his ass, firing the 10mm with both hands as she rushed forward; she hit the gunman four more times before he hit the ground. No sooner than he hit the ground, Vida was standing over him firing rounds into his head.

Even in the heat of the shoot out, Tonio saw Vida's work and gave her a look that read, Damn, ma!

Vida needed a way to vent her hurt and pain, the gunfight had awakened a dark side of her that hadn't reared its violent head in a long time.

The remaining gunman didn't stand a chance. Still trying to make a run for the door, he was gunned down by Tonio and Tia. The body fell right in front of the door, riddled with bullets.

Silence fell upon the store, in a creepy way. The strong smell of gunpowder filled the air. For a second, no one moved—it was as if time was standing still. As the smoke cleared, terrified customers slowly uncovered their heads and looked around. They began to get off the floor and run for the door in fear. They had to step over the dead bodies along the way.

Smoking 10mm in hand, Vida looked around to make sure Tia was okay.

Tia was fine.

Tonio looked at Born who was standing in the middle of the store with his smoking glock in hand, and said, "You okay, son?"

Born nodded, breathing hard, looking at Vida and Tia in amazement. He couldn't believe how they got down under pressure.

"I'm good, son, I'm good."

Looking around the tore up store Tonio said, "We gotta get outta here, we can't be here when jake show up."

"You right." Born said as he rushed over and snatched the mask off one of the dead gunmen. He didn't know him. Moving on quickly, he snatched the mask off of the other gunman. He didn't know him either but recognized his face from Jefferson Avenue.

They both nodded.

"We gotta be long gone before the law get here." Tia said.

The girl that ran the store, Niya, was balled up in the corner, shaking and crying—scared to death. Tonio rushed over to comfort her. Hugging her, he said, "You okay?"

Slowly, she nodded her head. "Yeah…"

"You gon' be just fine, I promise." Tonio said, rubbing her arms. "I need you to be strong and try to pull yourself together, okay?"

"Okay." She nodded.

"We gotta get outta here. I need you to tell the police it was a shoot out and all you know is that the other guys got away. You can't remember anything else because you were on the floor. Okay?"

Taking a deep breath, Niya said, "Okay." She was from the projects. Once she got herself together she would be fine.

Looking at Born, Tonio said, "Get outta here. I'll call you when I get where I'm goin'… We'll figure out what's next then."

Born popped a fresh clip in his Glock.

"I'ma make sure we get to the bottom of this!" He took off through the back of the store.

Looking at Vida and Tia, Tonio nodded toward the back office.

"Come on y'all, follow me."

The girls followed Tonio.

Inside Tonio's jet black Cadillac Escalade a short while later, he, Vida and Tia headed for his New Jersey house. One of three he had in the area. The New Jersey house was a safe house of sorts, no one knew about it but his brother, Daddieo, and Born.

In the back seat of the truck looking out the window, still nervous, Vida's mind was racing. She and Tia seemed to be running into one bad situation after the next. It felt like a dark cloud was following them—all odds were against them.

Looking over her shoulder to make sure they weren't being followed, Tia said, "Tonio, what the fuck you got goin' on up here?"

Tonio checked the rear view mirror and said, "I really ain't sure yet. I just learned that somebody got a hit out on me."

Vida sighed.

Tia did also. "We can't win for losin'." Tia rubbed her forehead. "Just our luck we walk right into some shit like this."

Vida shook her head. "I'm hip." She checked the clip in her 10mm. Only three bullets remained.

Tonio glanced at Tia, who was riding shotgun, and said, "I can't call it right now. I'ma get to the bottom of it though, you can bet that, ma."

Tia let out a frustrated laugh and said, "You got your hands full up here, Tonio. Me and Vida only gon' add to your problems."

Tonio looked at Tia like she was crazy.

"Come on, ma. I got love for you and Vida. That shit that went down back there gon' get taken care of ASAP, don't even trip. For real, I'm glad you and Vida was on the scene." Tonio looked back at Vida through the rear view and said, "Vida, you had that fire in your eyes back there."

"No bullshit," Tia added. "You zoned the fuck out. What was that all about, boo?"

Vida shrugged. "Gotta lot on my mind, I guess. Feel like I ain't got nothin' else to lose, you know?"

Tia nodded sympathetically. "I feel you, Vee."

"Me, too." Tonio said. His mind was still on the hit. Although he remained calm, he was pissed off.

"Y'all don't gotta worry 'bout nothin'. I got a spot for y'all to lay low until I can make somethin' happen for you."

"Can you really help us disappear?" Vida asked Tonio.

"Like I said," Tonio rubbed his chin, "money will get you anything you-"

"Damn!" Tia snapped.

Tonio and Vida gave her wild looks.

Tia looked back at Vida and said, "Our money still in the car, we need that."

"What money?" Tonio asked.

Tia told Tonio that the $75,000 she and Vida had was in the trunk of the car they were driving.

"Don't worry about that, ma." Tonio waved his hand. "I'll get Niya to watch the car 'til I send somebody to get it. I got you."

Tia sighed with relief.

"Good, cause that's all the money we got."

"Are you sure you can help us wit' all the shit you got goin' on?" Vida said changing the subject.

"Vida," Tonio looked at her through the rearview. "I'm a gangsta, for real. I got this shit under control. Let me do this, you and Tia in good hands. Trust me."

Tonio's words were comforting for Vida and Tia. He was their ace in the hole at the time.

Rubbing her hand through her hair, Tia said, "If we can get out country we gon' be 'aight, joe, for real."

"I can make it happen. I got a cousin on the run right now... been on the run for ten years." Tonio said.

Vida raised her eyebrows. She was all ears.

"What he on the run for?" She asked.

"Killed a bank teller and shot a cop in a bank robbery in the 90s... got away wit' five-hundred thousand and disappeared. He been on *America's Most Wanted* and all that shit. A friend of mine put the shit in motion and got my cousin to South America—Brazil somewhere."

Tia smiled. "That's what the fuck I'm talkin' 'bout, slim."

"How long will it take to put that in motion?" Vida said.

"No more than two weeks." Tonio said as the Jay-Z ring tone on his cell phone cut into the conversation. He checked the number; it was Born.

"Hold on y'all, give me a second. It's, Born." He flipped the phone open. "Yeah, son." Tonio answered.

"I ain't gon' rap too much, but I done put the shit together. I just want you to know that." Born said.

"Meet me at my Jersey spot."

"Bet." Born ended the call.

Tonio shut his phone and put it in his pocket.

Tia saw the look on Tonio's face and said, "What's good?"

"Born know, or think he know, what the hell's going on."

Vida cut in and said, "Well you can get rid of the problem then, right?"

"That's the game plan." Tonio said as they crossed the George Washington Bridge into New Jersey.

"Like you said, you's a gangsta." Vida said. "It's chess, not checkers. Play for keeps."

Tonio nodded in agreement. "You right… it's chess, not checkers…" His mind was working over time. He wanted to make his next move his best move. If Born was on to something, Tonio planned to strike fast.

Tia cut the TV on in the visor. The shoot out at Tonio's store was already on the news. No real information
was being given out. Good.

Tonio glanced at the TV and shook his head with a
sigh.

Inside Tonio's Teaneck, New Jersey house, Vida and
Tia were in the kitchen eating KFC fried chicken. Tonio
and Born were in the living room talking about the drama
at hand. As far as Born was concerned, a major drug figure by the name of, Romel was behind the hit on Tonio
and the shooting at the store. The dead gunman that Born
recognized from Jefferson Avenue was down with Romel's crew. It took Born a while to put it all together in
his head but after a little thought it all made sense. Tonio
and Romel weren't really comrades; they met through
another Harlem drug dealer by the name of, Boogie who
had love for them both.

Boogie was a throw back nigga that wanted everybody to eat. He put Tonio and Romel down with his Mex-
ican drug connect. Month's later Boogie was murdered in
a broad daylight hit on him at his barbershop. Romel had
Boogie's killers murdered within days. Afterwards, Romel and Tonio continued to cop from the same drug connect, putting their money together to get more product for
less money.

Sitting on the sofa rubbing his chin in deep thought as
Born explained everything to him, Tonio was pissed off at

92

the thought that Romel could have such a wicked plot in effect.

"You know what, it makes sense, Born. If Romel gets me out the way he'll have the connect all to himself and couldn't nobody really get in his way."

"Make no mistake about it." Born said. "Son, on everything I love, as far as I'm concerned, Romel coulda been behind that move with' Boogie gettin' killed."

Rubbing his chin, nodding his head, Tonio said, "You got a point, son. You got a good point there." Tonio paused for a second in deep thought. He was supposed to meet Romel so they could holla at the connect together, now Tonio was thinking about taking Romel out.

Born could tell what was going through Tonio's mind.

"Yo, son, don't even think about it, just let me take care of this shit—it's time to clean house." Born's voice was full of conviction. He was ready to let his gun go.

With a nod, Tonio said, "Fuck it, let's make it happen... do your thing."

Born stood up to leave. "Watch how I do this, son. I got you."

"I know." Tonio dug deep inside his pocket and pulled out a set of car keys. He tossed the keys to Born. "Get somebody to move that car Vida and Tia left parked in front of the store. Have them park it behind the store and get the bag of money out the trunk. You bring the money here to me. Cool?"

"I got you, Tonio. Ain't no thing. But look here... I want you to stay put until I can really put this in motion."

"You know what? Don't even worry 'bout it… I know what I wanna do. I want you to take out Romel today, I'll set up a-"

Tonio's cell phone cut him off. He pulled out the phone and saw it was Romel calling looking at Born, Tonio said, "This the nigga Romel right here."

"See what he talkin' 'bout." Born raised his eyebrows.

Tonio answered the phone. "What's good, son?"

Tonio, I can't meet you today somethin' just came up. We gon have to put that off for a day or two, okay, son?"

Tonio's mind was dead-set on killing Romel at this point. He looked at Born and gave him a deadly nod. "Aye, Romel, is everything aight wit' you?"

"Yeah, just got a little business to take care of. You know how shit come up in these streets." Romel sounded nervous.

"Say no more, I'll give you a call in a day or two, son." Tonio ended the call and looked at Born. "We need to put this nigga in the dirt fast."

In the kitchen at the table eating fried chicken, Vida and Tia were talking about how life could be if they got out of the country.

Taking a bite, Tia said, "Where would we go, Vee?"

"China for all I care." Vida joked. "Anywhere is better than a fuckin' prison cell, feel me?"

Tia laughed. "For real though, what about Mexico or Canada. I'm sure it won't be hard to get to one of them spots."

"We'll see. Let's see what Tonio can come up wit'."

Tia nodded. "You right, we'll play it by ear."

Tonio walked into the kitchen with a stressful look on his handsome face.

"Y'all might as well get comfortable. We gon' lay low here for a day or two while my peoples take care of a few things on the streets. Cool?"

"Cool." Tia said.

"I already made a few phone calls about fresh IDs for you two… I also sent Born to get the money y'all left in the car."

"Thanks, Tonio." Vida said.

"Don't mention it, ma." Tonio took a seat and grabbed a piece of chicken. He bit right into it.

"So Tonio, what's good wit' your situation? You on top of it… you know who wants you dead?" Tia said.

Tonio slightly nodded. "I'm pretty sure I know who's behind the hit. I got my peoples on his ass right now. Don't even worry 'bout it."

Tia smiled. Streets niggas, ones about their business, turned her on.

"That's right, big slim. Handle your business." Tia said.

Tonio and Vida laughed.

Switching gears, Vida said, "Aye, Tonio, me and Tee was wondering what other country we could make it to."

Enjoying another piece of chicken, Tonio said, "It's a number of spots… Panama… somewhere in Mexico, somewhere like that. The world is huge. Don't even worry 'bout that. Let me deal with all of that."

Vida nodded. "Aight, that's cool wit' me."

"Me, too." Tia said.

Standing up Tonio said, "Make your selves at home. I need a shower." He left the kitchen feeling the weight of the world on his shoulders.

About an hour later, Tonio was sitting on the sofa in the basement watching ESPN as he sipped a glass of Hennessy. A few "E" pills sat on the coffee table beside a small pile of purple haze. Tonio wasn't fucked up, but he was super nice. In nothing but a pair of Polo boxers, he was chillin' trying to clear his mind. Thoughts of the hit on his life had his full attention.

"Aye, Tonio." Tia came down the steps in gray sweats and a white T-shirt, looking sexy as shit. She laid eyes on Tonio's body and was turned on by his chest and abs. He was in great shape. "Damn, you down here wit' no clothes on and shit."

Tonio smiled. "A man can do that in his own house, can't he?"

"By all means." Tia smiled. She couldn't help but to notice the large bulge in his boxers. Damn, he got a big ass dick, she thought.

"Anyway, I wanted to know if you got some smoke, but I see that you do." She walked over and took a seat beside him. Although she played it off well, she was turned on and felt a surprising wetness between her thighs.

Tonio handed Tia a Dutch and said, "Roll something up."

"You ain't gotta say it twice, champ." Tia grabbed some of the haze and began rolling it.

"Where Vida at?" Tonio asked.

"Sleep, she stressin'." Tia laid eyes on the "E" pills and wanted one.

"What about you, how you holdin' up? I know y'all been through a world of shit wit' everything that's goin' on." Tonio sipped some Hennessy and popped a pill.

Tia shrugged. "I'm sayin'… I'm fucked up. We lost Moe-Moe and Bloody back to back in a matter of hours. We on the run…and I damn sure ain't gon' sit in nobody's prison. Fuck that. I'm numb, I feel real cold inside, Tonio. But on the real, I'm more worried 'bout Vida. She ain't the same no more, a part of her died wit' Moe-Moe."

"I feel you on that."

Tia finished rolling the Dutch and licked the tip. "Gimme a light."

Tonio pulled a lighter from the pocket of his Gucci jeans on the floor. "Here you go." He lit the Dutch and watched Tia puff it to life. The strong smell lit up the basement.

Tonio and Tia passed the Dutch back and forth as they spoke about the drama at hand. Slowly, the purple haze had them both on Mars.

"What the hell is that?!" Tia's eyes grew wide with astonishment as she pointed at the source of her amazement.

Tonio was rock hard. His erection came out of no-where like a quiet storm. It was trying to fight its way out of his Polo boxers, all ten inches of his manhood.

Looking down at his dick, not trying to hide his erection, Tonio said, "What can I say, you turn a nigga on, ma."

"Uhunuhn," Tia covered her mouth with a smile and shook her head. He was so big, bigger than she thought when she first took a quick look. Now that she was twisted, he looked larger than life. The wetness between her thighs was spreading with every passing second.

With a smooth smile on his face, Tonio said, "You act surprised."

"You are huge." She was clearly impressed.

"You sexy as shit." He reached over and rubbed his hand through her sexy, short haircut. He could smell the Dove soap on her skin.

Tia closed her eyes, enjoying his touch. It sent chills through her body.

"I'm wet as shit." She whispered, opening and closing her legs. There was a fire burning between them.

"I'm hard as shit, so what's next?" Tonio joked.

"You got a rubber?" She took a deep breath.

"Yeah, I'll be right back, ma." Tonio got up and head-ed to the bathroom with his erection leading the way.

Tia popped an "E" pill and washed it down with a swallow of Hennessy. She sat back and waited for Tonio to return. When Tonio came out of the bathroom with a pack of rubbers, Tia watched his huge dick all the way across the room. She planned to enjoy it and as high as she was, she knew it'd be good.

In a sexy way, Tia looked up at Tonio and whispered, "I always wanted to holla at you." She reached out and stoked his manhood without pulling it out of his boxers. He felt even larger than he looked inside her small hand. She closed her eyes and leaned her face forward and rubbed her face against his manhood from side to side. The "E" was in full effect; it had Tia's sex drive on 1000. Sexy moans began to escape her mouth.

Tonio whispered, "Take your clothes off, ma. I wanna see your body."

Tia smiled. Her eyes were damn near shut she was so high. Smoothly, she took her clothes off piece by piece. She never took her eyes off of Tonio's erection. When she was done undressing she dangled her white thong from her fingertips.

"I'm all yours, now what's up?" She dropped her thong on the floor.

Tonio came out of his boxers and dropped them on the floor. With his hands on his waist, he stood right in Tia's face letting her enjoy the sight of his strong erection. He then got down on his knees, slowly, and pushed Tia's legs apart.

"Your pussy hair is so neat…" He looked up and saw Tia playing with her hard nipples.

The phone rang and they both jumped.

Tonio said, "Fuck that phone."

"Yeah, fuck that phone."

Tonio slid a finger inside her tight wetness. It was hot and so tight. She moaned as he slipped another finger inside her and began to stroke her for a few seconds.

Dying to get inside Tia's tight pussy, Tonio stopped what he was doing and grabbed a rubber. The phone stopped ringing as he tore the rubber out of the pack and put it on.

"Come here, ma." He pulled Tia to him and gave her a deep kiss. They hugged. His dick smashed against her stomach. Their hands let the "E" pills take control as they felt all over each other.

Breathing hard, Tonio said, "Turn around."

Tia turned around and bent over on the sofa. Tonio slid inside her from the back—it was so wet and tight. She moaned as he inched inside of her. Deeper and deeper until he had given her his all, and then he began to stroke her. Nice and long. He gripped her hips.

"Ah, Tonio…Ah yeah…Ah yeah… Tonio…It's so good…. So…Ah…So big, Tonio." Tia dug her nails into the sofa as Tonio filled her insides like a plumber laying pipe. With every plunge inside Tia's wet pussy he pulled her to him by her hips. Wet, sopping sounds came from her pussy; that was turning Tonio on even more. They were both in another world of sexual bliss.

"I always wanted to fuck you, Tia."

With her eyes closed, throwing the pussy back at Tonio, Tia moaned, "Is it what you thought it would be?"

"Ahh, better, so much better, so much tighter than I thought." Tonio began to put more back into it, digging deeper inside of Tia, hitting all the right spots. Tia's moans grew louder with every satisfying stroke. Her pussy got wetter with every long stroke.

"I'm about to cum, oh my God, I'm about to cum so hard…fuck me…Fuck me, Tonio." Tia squeezed her pussy as tight as she could around Tonio's dick. She moaned with deep pleasure.

"Oh Shit…Oh shit…you fuckin' the shit out of me, so good…so so good." Tia's eyes rolled back in her head as she bit down on her bottom lip. She still made vicious fuck sounds as if she was taking the best dick she ever had.

Minutes on the clock flew by in a blur as they fucked with strong passion. Tia's first orgasm was atomic and caused her whole body to shake.

Looking down at Tia's pretty ass, Tonio smacked it hard.

"Ssssss…" Tia hissed. "Do that again. Ahhhh…Ssss, yeah, I like that."

Tonio smiled. Sweat was dripping down his face. Both of their bodies were covered with sex-sweat. He reached for her nipple. Tia came again, moaning from deep within her soul. Tonio enjoyed her explosion as much as she did.

"I'm 'bout to cum, Tia." Tonio grunted as he began to fuck her with urgency.

"Oh yea, I like it like that…Fuck me harder…Let me know you there, make it hurt!"

Tonio closed his eyes, gritted his teeth, gripped Tia's hips firmly, and began slamming up inside her pussy with force, over and over and over again.

"Shhhhit, you fuckin' the…. Ummm…you fuckin' the shit out of me…you so damn hard and big."

Tonio grunted and growled as he came with force. "Ahhh, damn, girl…"

Breathing hard, they both slowed down. Tonio pulled out of her pussy. They both flopped down on the sofa, trying to catch their breath.

Looking at each other, they both laughed.

Tonio said, "Damn, I needed that."

"You? It was right on time for me, too." Tia smiled. "That shit kills stress."

Tonio laughed. "No Bullshit, ma."

The Hunt

It was just getting dark in D.C. Drama was in the air like a thick fog. Everybody had heard about the beef between Most Wanted and Hell Razor. The streets were saying that Most Wanted got out on Hell Razor. Paris was pissed off when she heard this, her anger only grew more when she and her girls couldn't find any Most Wanted Honies in the streets. Nevertheless, Paris was dead-set on punishing them.

Inside Paris' car, she, Tera, and Lala were riding up 19th street, passing the Stadium Armory. They'd just come from around Potomac Gardens looking for Summer and Bria. Paris had got word that Summer and Bria were hanging out around the Gardens talking shit about the Hell Razor Honeys. However, Summer and Bria were nowhere to be found. Now Paris and her girls were headed around Kenilworth Avenue to see if they could run into any Most Wanted Honies.

They rode nodding her head to the sounds of T.I.'s, "You Don't Know Me", that was pumpin' through the speakers.

"Them bitches duckin' us now. We been lookin' for these bitches all day long. They know what the fuck is up." Tera said.

Behind the wheel, Paris sucked her teeth and said, "I ain't doin' no fightin' at all. I'ma show these bitches what time it is." She had a small .380 automatic on her lap. Lala was in the back seat sending text messages back and forth with Driver. She was really feeling him but wouldn't think about letting Paris, Tera, or any of the other Hell Razor Honeys know her true feelings. She really wasn't feeling what Paris was talking about as far as gunplay. Lala was cool with fucking a bitch up, but Paris was now talking about smoking a bitch and Lala wasn't too sure about that. Thinking about all the heat Vida and Tia had on them made Lala seriously question Paris's attitude. She knew Paris hated being questioned so Lala kept her feelings to herself.

Sensing a funny vibe from Lala, Paris looked at her through the rear view mirror and said, "Aye, Lala, what's up? Why you so quiet?"

"Ain't nothin' just thinkin'." Lala said.

"'Bout what?" Paris pressed.

Lala sighed. Paris had a way of pulling information out of people.

"Well, on the real, we ridin' 'round lookin' for these Most Wanted bitches so we can fuck' em up, but now you talkin' 'bout guns and murder and shit...That ain't no lightweight shit there, you know."

Tera looked back at Lala with raised eyebrows and a confused expression on her face. Tera wasn't a killer, but she was with whatever Paris wanted to do.

"Lala, you got shit twisted. Them bitches jumped out there and we gon' deal wit' they ass. They gon' respect Hell Razor, believe that." Paris said.

Tera added her two cents by saying, "They deserve all they got comin'. You sound like you second guessin' and shit. Like you ain't down for the struggle or somethin'."

Feeling pressured by her girls, Lala snapped.

"I'm down for the struggle!" she shouted. "I'm down for whatever! All I said is murder ain't no lightweight shit! That's all I said…Shit! I got a brother doin' life for murder so I ain't gon' take the shit lightly."

Paris rolled her eyes and sighed as if she wasn't feeling Lala.

"You ain't the only bitch in this car that got family doin' life—that shit come wit' the streets. I don't plan to get caught for nothin' I do. Them Most Wanted bitches drew blood and they gon' pay for that. Don't nobody fuck wit' us. Period! Either you wit' us or you ain't, Lala."

An awkward silence fell upon the car for a moment. Paris, Tera, and Lala were closer than blood sisters, but when they disagreed with one another it always seemed to get heated. Although, Lala was never the one to stand against Paris, most of the time it was Tera. Nevertheless, Lala had spoken her mind.

"Look y'all," Lala said, "Do you see all the shit Vida and them is caught up in? Is that what you want, Paris?"

Lala's words made Tera think for a second. By no means did she want that kind of heat on her, but at the same time she was down to ride.

With a quick response, Paris fired back, "Vida and them killed a police, that's way different! We beefin' wit' some bitches on the streets."

Giving in and frustrated, Lala threw her hands in the air and said, "Fuck it, it's whatever."

Tera sighed.

"Paris, I don't know Lala kinda got a point. We need to be smart about whatever we do."

Paris cut her eyes at Tera and burst out laughing.

"I know your shit-startin'-ass ain't trippin' off smokin' some bitches."

Tera smiled. She was known for being a shit-starter.

"I'm just sayin', Vida and them been all on the news and some more shit...we don't want that kind of heat. You know?"

"Look y'all!" Paris was done talking. "We gon' let them bitches have it, they gon' know we mean business!" She had fire in her eyes. "If that mean puttin' a bullet in one of them bitches then so be it!"

Tera shrugged. "Let's make it happen then."

Lala sighed silently and looked out the window at the Southeast streets.

A short while later, go-go music was blasting inside of the blue BMW 335 that was parked in the far corner of the 7-Eleven parking lot on the Rhode Island Avenue. Summer, Bria, and their girl Ne'Shelle were inside the BMW talking about how they had stepped to the Hell Razor Honeys earlier. They knew that it was now "on sight" with Hell Razor, and they were ready for whatever. Personally, Summer was glad that shit had come to a head between Most Wanted and Hell Razor. She felt that Hell

Razor Honeys were way too overrated in the streets. Summer couldn't stand Paris anyway.

Looking at her slick ass Gucci watch, Summer looked back at her girl Ne'Shelle in the back seat and said, "Call Cee-Cee again, she shoulda been up here by now."

Calling Cee-Cee on her cell phone, Ne'Shelle said, "I don't know what's takin' her so long...She said she was a few minutes away." Ne'Shelle got Cee-Cee on the phone and spoke to her for a few seconds. Ending the call, Ne'Shelle said, "Aye, Summer, Cee-Cee and them a few blocks away. She said they got pulled over by the police."

Summer raised her eyebrows and said, "Oh yeah?"

"That's what she said." Ne'Shelle nodded, looking out the window at two fly-ass niggas walking by.

Sitting in the passenger seat playing with a deadly switchblade, Bria said, "I'm tryin' to hit the go-go tonight. What y'all tryin' to do?"

Ne'Shelle laughed.

"I don't know about you bitches, but I'm tryin' to get some pills and some hard dick for the night."

All the girls busted out laughing.

Summer said, "I know that's right, Shelle. I don't know... I might hit the go-go tonight, but I know we gon' run into them Hell Razor bitches so it's gon' be drama."

Bria nodded. "You already know that, but it's whatever. Them bitches don't want it for real. They livin' off Vida and Tia and 'nem name, actin' like they go like the old Hell Razor Honeys. Ain't nobody stuntin' that weak-ass shit."

"No bullshit." Ne'Shelle said.

The sound of a car pulling into the parking lot caught the girls' attention. They thought it was Cee-Cee for a second. They were wrong. It was Paris, Tera and Lala in Paris' Honda Civic. Ne'Shelle turned all the way around in her seat to make sure it was who she thought it was.

"Aye, y'all, that's them Hell Razor bitches right there!"

Bria gripped the switchblade tight and said, "I wish them bitches would act like they want some more work."

Summer pulled a box cutter from her Prada bag and said, "We gon' cut these bitches up this time." She opened her door to get out. "Let's punish these bitches."

Summer got out of the car followed by Bria and Ne'Shelle.

Paris stopped her car in the middle of the parking lot and threw it in park.

"Look at these fake-ass bitches." She had a smirk on her face.

Getting out of the Civic, Tera said, "These bitches act like they really want it!"

She was ready to punish some shit. She was already pissed off that she wasn't outside when Most Wanted came through Saratoga Avenue the first time. Tera loved drama, she lived for it.

Paris and Lala jumped out of the car right behind Tera.

Leading her crew toward the Hell Razor Honeys, Summer shouted, "You bitches just don't get enough, huh?!"

Ne'Shelle chimed in as well. "I think these bitches freaks for pain."

A few bystanders in front of the 7-Eleven saw the drama about to explode and swiftly continued on their way.

Tera saw the weapons the Most Wanted Honies had and pulled out a box cutter of her own. "Ain't that cute, y'all got a knife and some box cutters... I'm scared to death."

With her hands behind her back, letting the Most Wanted Honies walk up on her and her crew, Paris gave up and evil smile.

"Well, what y'all waitin' for? Let's do the damn thing."

Summer was about five feet away from Paris when she said, "I'm sick of your mouth bitch, you all talk for real!"

Paris' smile faded as she pulled the .380 from behind her back and aimed at Summer's face. "Bitch, picture me bein' all talk."

Tera and Lala looked at Paris like she was crazy. It was a number of people inside and outside of the 7-Eleven. All eyes were on the girls in the parking lot.

Summer and her crew stopped dead in their tracks. Their eyes were wide with fear.

With the .380 aimed at Summer's face, Paris looked in the eyes of all three Most Wanted Honies and said, "I don't hear you bitches runnin' your fuckin' mouth now!" She had a mean smirk on her face. It was clear that her mind was on murder.

Summer, Bria, and Ne'Shelle gave each other quick glances and took off running like Paris was already shooting at them. They ran in different directions.

Paris opened fire with five quick shots.

"Don't run! Dirty-ass bitches!" She was aiming at Summer's head.

Summer, Bria, and Ne'Shelle made it behind parked cars, ducking bullets.

The gunfire sent bystanders running in all directions in fear of a stray bullet.

Paris ran after Summer, firing round after round as if she had an extended clip. She didn't have an extended clip, her thirteen rounds were done in seconds, leaving her with an empty pistol. Out of bullets, Paris took off running for her car. Tera and Lala did the same.

A white Acura TSX skidded into the 7-Eleven parking lot with screeching tires. The car came to a stop and the driver's side door flew open. Cee-Cee jumped out looking like Hoopz off the show, *Flavor of Love*. Cee-Cee fired shots from her 9mm at Paris's car as the Civic took off flying out of the parking lot like a racecar.

Peeking from behind a parked car across the street from the 7-Eleven, Summer saw Cee-Cee firing her pistol. As much as she hated for Cee-Cee to always ride around with a pistol, Summer was so happy that Cee-Cee had showed up with a pistol this time. Scared to death, Summer breathed a sigh of relief.

The Hideout

Hours later, Tia was taking a hot shower in Tonio's master bathroom. She and Tonio had taken fucking to new heights with the assistance of ecstasy and purple haze. Satisfied sexually, still high and horny as shit, Tia closed her eyes and let the hot water relax her body. Her problems were worlds away. Tonio had made her feel so good. Never was she one to let the dick cloud her judgment, or take her mind off what was important, but at the moment she was enjoying her high and the sexual thoughts of how Tonio took her over the edge again and again in his basement.

Damn, that shit was so good, Tia thought as she turned around to let the hot water pound on her back like a water-pressure-massage. Thinking of Tonio she touched herself. Her clit was still extremely sensitive, she was still rollin' off the pill and smoke. As soon as she rubbed her clit her legs began to tremble. She closed her eyes again and bit her bottom lip. Her free hand found her left breast and began to squeeze it. A low moan came from deep within. Her fingers played with her pussy and hard nipple as if her hands belonged to Tonio. An orgasm was right around the corner, she could feel it coming quickly like a strong wind. Under the hot water she jerked and shook as she moved her head side-to-side with erotic thoughts flooding her mind. Self-pleasuring was not something Tia was used to, but the ecstasy made it feel so good and natural to her at the moment.

Flames grew out of control between her legs as her wetness grew. Her fingers were hard at work, making love to herself. She wanted to cum again, bad. The way she came off of the "E" and purple haze was like no other orgasm she'd ever felt and she was dying for that kind of orgasm one more time. Maybe two, or three more times.

She worked her clit with her finger like the expert tongue of a great lover. She moaned softly. The hot steam that filled the bathroom had nothing on the sexual heat between her legs. Her whole body began to tingle. She went from one breast to the other with her free hand, pinching her wet hard nipples. The sexual sensations were out of this world, they were too strong. Her orgasm was seconds away. Her fingers slid in and out of her gushing pussy faster and faster.

"Oh...Ahhh...Sss...Damn." She came so hard. "Ahhh..." She continued to work her pussy. Moments later, after the first orgasm was gone, a stronger one hit her like a truck.

"Oh my, God." Her knees got weak. Back-to-back orgasms attacked her and made her moan as if she had a yard of dick inside her.

"Mmmmmmm," She hummed, enjoying the dying, body-shaking orgasm.

Alone in one of the guest rooms of Tonio's house, Vida had too much on her mind. Thoughts of Moe-Moe, and thoughts of Bloody. Thoughts of being on the run and feeling like the walls were closing in on her. The weight of her stress was heavy. She couldn't get it off her mind.

The flat screen TV that hung from the wall was on BET, but Vida wasn't paying it any attention. She had found a copy of, "The 48 Laws of Power", on Tonio's coffee table and got into the book. The laws in the book had her thinking of a number of ways to accomplish one goal or another while living life on the run.

A light knock at the door grabbed Vida's attention.

"Yeah, what's up?" She said.

The door slowly opened and Tia stuck her head in.

"You okay? You been in here by yourself for hours…I'm just checkin' on my girl."

Vida flashed a weak smile.

"I'm cool, Tee, just tryin' to get my thoughts together."

Tia nodded, understandingly as she walked over and sat on the bed beside Vida. She knew Vida so well that she could tell what was on her mind; she didn't have to ask. The look in Vida's eyes spoke volumes. She was still in pain about Moe-Moe and Bloody. Not to mention being on the run for murder.

Closing the book she was reading, Vida said, "You look twisted."

With a smirk on her cute face, Tia said, "I'm high as shit. I had to do somethin' to calm my nerves." She told Vida how she smoked weed and popped some "E" with Tonio in the basement and how they did some good old

113

fashion fucking after that. There was no shame in her game; Tia always kept it gangsta.

Vida smiled and shook her head at Tia.

"That's one way to clear your mind." She joked.

Tia laughed.

"You got some more weed? I need to ease my nerves my damn self."

"It's some more haze in the basement...I'll go get you some."

Vida stood up and stretched.

"Nah, I'll go down there wit' you, I gotta use the bathroom first." She slipped on her black and red Gucci tennis shoes.

"So was the dick any good?"

"What?!" Tia laughed.

"The dick...was it any good?" Vida was serious.

"I was high as shit, but it was on one thousand, I give 'em that." Tia smiled.

Vida gave up a small laugh. "Well, it was worth it then."

Tia nodded. "Yeah, it was worth it."

"You might've fucked our chances up as far as gettin' out the country." Vida joked.

"Why you say that, Vee?"

"You threw that good pussy on his ass, you know how niggas is about that good shit—they be wantin' to keep it close."

Tia died laughing. A good strong laugh. Vida got a good laugh out of that as well. They needed a good laugh.

Overcoming the laughter, Tia looked at Vida and said, "Vee, we gon' be alright…we gon' get far away from here and never look back."

Nodding her head, Vida said, "I hope so."

Tia got up and gave Vida a firm hug. Looking her in the eyes, Tia said, "Vee! We gon' be 'aight… It's only one way to look at it."

"You right… It's gon' be aight." Vida had her doubts, but she had to make herself believe that things would work out for the best.

A short while later, Tonio came into the house with a stressful look on his face. He shut the door behind him and activated the alarm system. Heading toward the living room he made a quick phone call on his cell phone. After a few quick words he ended the call and took a seat on the sofa and rubbed his forehead. He was in thought.

"Damn, I ain't know you came back already." Tia said, coming down the steps.

Looking over his shoulder, Tonio smiled. "I just stepped in." He sounded frustrated.

"What's up? Why you look like that?" Tia sat on the sofa with a little space between her and Tonio. They didn't act like two people that had just had mind-blowing sex hours ago.

"Born and three of my men just got locked up." Tonio shook his head with a long sigh. "They got popped with a bunch of guns and vest."

"Damn," Tia shook her head.

"They was on their way to hit the nigga that put the hit on me." Tonio told Tia about he situation with Romel. "I gotta get this nigga out the way, Tia. He playin' a deadly game and I ain't got time to play around wit' a snake like this nigga here."

Tia nodded. "I feel you. So what's your next move?"

Before Tonio could answer, his cell vibrated. He checked the number and answered the phone. The conversation lasted a few moments. Ending the call, Tonio looked at Tia and said, "I got IDs and passports for you and Vida...They'll be ready in two days."

Tia smiled. "Just like that?"

"Money talks, you know that." Tonio shrugged.

"You my nigga." Tia gave him a tight hug.

"Oh yeah, I got that money y'all left in the car, too. It's in my truck."

"Thanks." Tia was grateful. "I knew you'd come through for us. I told Vee you'd look out for us."

"I got love for y'all, it ain't nothin'. You know that." Tonio rubbed his chin, still thinking about Born and his other men. Their arrest was a heavy blow. Yet and still, Romel was still a major problem that had to be dealt with.

"Where the hell we gon' go wit' the passports, Tonio? We ain't got nothin' mapped out."

"I'll take care of all that, ma. Don't even stunt that."

Tonio's phone vibrated again. He checked to see who was calling and answered the phone.

"Yeah, what's good, son?"

Tia paid close attention to the conversation Tonio was having. She could tell that it was serious by the look on his face.

Moments later, Tonio ended the call and sat his phone on the glass table in front of him. For a second he didn't say a word, just sat there in deep thought.

"What's up?" Tia raised her eyebrows.

With a sigh, Tonio said, "I know where the nigga at that put the money on my head."

"The bamma, Romel?"

"Yeah, but wit' Born and them gettin' bagged I really can't handle shit the way I want to. I can't just walk up in the spot and handle the shit on some gangsta shit... I gotta be smooth wit' it."

"Where the nigga at?"

"Son at this club called the Silver Bullet. It would be a perfect time to get his ass, too."

"Why?"

"'Cause he out in the open but I only trust born wit' shit like that." Tonio rubbed his chin, thinking about calling on one of his young guns to do the hit.

With a slight shrug Tia said, "Shit, don't nobody know me like that up here...I could take care of that for you and couldn't nobody connect the shit to you. Consider it a favor for a favor, one hand washin' the other. What the fuck, me and Vida should be out the country in a few days anyway, right?"

Tonio gave Tia a look like he was really thinking about what she was throwing his way. After a few seconds of thought a broad smile crossed his face.

"You gangsta as shit, ma."

"It's a D.C. thing, what can I say?"

"You got a good idea. You damn sure could pull it off. A sexy-ass shortie like you...a nigga would never see it comin'."

"I'm hip, I'm tryin' to put you on point." Tia was on to something. Romel was a huge trick. A pretty face like Tia's would get him to put his guards down with no problem.

Tonio turned toward Tia and said, "It's one problem though, ma, you can't hit the nigga in the club. He gon' have too many people with him."

"I feel you, but I know how to operate. I been doin' this shit since I was a youngin', Tonio."

Tonio smiled. "Cool, I want you to slide up on the nigga and work that sexy D.C. magic on his ass just to get his attention-"

Tia rolled her eyes with a smile and cut Tonio off.

"Look, slim, just get me a clean pistol and show me where the nigga at. I got it from there. That's on everything."

Tonio gave Tia a look of admiration for a second, thinking things over. She could pull it off, he was sure of it. With a slow nod, Tonio said, "Cool, let me make a phone call and put a few things in motion to make sure you safe inside the club." He paused for a second and then said, "How Vida gon' feel 'bout this?"

"Feel about what?" Vida bent the corner and stepped into the room with her eyebrows raised.

Tia and Tonio were surprised.

Tia explained the whole situation to Vida. Being as though Tonio had already secured IDs and passports for

Tia and Vida, Tia felt that it would only be fair to handle the business for Tonio.

Vida felt uncertain about the move at first. They were already on the run.

"Tee, you know how I feel. If you wit' it, I'm wit' it. We got new IDs and passports, fuck it. Let's do it. You all I got left in this world, so you know I got your back. Til' death do us part."

Tia gave Vida five. "That's right, til' death do us part."

Tonio smiled, he knew Vida and Tia were perfect for the job.

The Target

The VIP section of the Silver Bullet was the place to be, by all means. 50 Cent and the whole G-Unit crew would be coming through shortly. The whole club was packed with ladies that were dying to get up close and personal with 50 or anybody else from G-Unit. Kanye's, "Diamonds from Sierra Leone", was blaring through the speakers that surrounded the VIP section. Weed smoke was thick in the air. Expensive bottles of Champagne were flowing freely—Busta Rhymes, DJ Drama, and record executive Steve Stoute were in the VIP section, it was clear that Romel was the center of attention. Women were all over him, bad ass women that looked like they were snatched off the set of Nelly's, "Tip Drill" video. The sexy women in the spot outnumbered the dudes ten to one. Everything was just the way Romel wanted it.

Romel was a Harlem nigga with a lot of pull in the streets. He was touching a nice piece of paper in the game and controlled countless blocks in the Harlem drug trade. Romel was a big dude, at 6'4 he could pass for a NFL player. Handsome with brown skin and a bright smile, Romel was what the ladies wanted in a man. He also had the respect of the streets. At 32, he had been on top of his game, took a fall, did five years in the feds and was back on top of his game. By all means, Romel played for keeps and lived by the code of the streets. Money was the center of his life and anything that got in his way had to go.

Off to the side, behind the bar, Romel was telling his man, Manny, how he was fucked up about the sloppy hit on Tonio.

"I told you to let me take care of that nigga Tonio, Romel." Manny said.

Romel sighed and shook his head.

"How many times I gotta tell you that if you make a move on Tonio the feds gon' come get us both and we gon' be sittin' in a fuckin' cage facin' murder charges? We don't need the heat."

"We got a problem now…Tonio ain't no fool. He gon' know what's up." Manny rubbed his chin.

"Don't worry 'bout that, I'm already on top of it." Romel looked around the VIP section at all the beautiful women. "Wit' Born and his goons out of the picture for a second, Tonio ain't got the muscle to move on me."

"Born ain't gon' lay down, Ro. Tonio's lawyer gon' have him out on bond in a few days." Manny said.

"A few days is all I need." Romel winked. "I got it under control." He gave Manny a pound, killing his drink and nodding at the passing Erick Sermon. "Anyway, we gon' enjoy the night and have a good time. We gon' be runnin' shit in a minute wit' Tonio out the picture."

121

The main area of the Silver Bullet was packed. 50 Cent was a big draw. Close to three hundred people were stuffed into a spot that was made to hold two hundred. G-Unit's, Tony Yayo, was on stage working the crowd, getting them ready for 50.

Making their way through the thick crowd looking like a million bucks, Tia and Vida were on a mission.

Yelling over the pounding music, Vida said, "Aye, Tee, I woulda felt better if we already had the pistols wit' us."

Vida and Tia went inside the club unarmed and were now looking for one of Tonio's people so they could get their hands on some heat to take care of business.

"I feel the same way, Vee but we 'aight." Tia said as she looked around the packed club. It was too packed for her liking and that had her irritable. "The quicker we smoke this nigga the quicker we can get the fuck on about our business. Wit' this shit out the way Tonio can focus all his energy on helpin' us. Feel me?"

Vida nodded in agreement as she kept her eyes on everything going on around her. She still felt uneasy about the situation, but was down whole-heartedly.

Vida and Tia made their way to the bar. Dudes were trying to holla at them left and right. A huge dark-skinned dude that was part of the security squad made eye contact with Tia, she gave him a slight nod and the security dude stepped off.

Vida saw the move and whispered to Tia, "That's the joker right there?"

"Yeah, that gotta be him." Tia said, checking out Tony Yayo on stage. A hot second later the cell phone that

Tonio had given to Tia vibrated. It was a text message telling her to make her way to the bathroom. "This us right here, I'll be right back wit' the hammers." Tia stepped off looking sexy as she threw her ass on her way through the crowd.

Playing with a razor in her mouth, Vida eyes the crowd carefully. Countless thoughts raced through her mind. Shit was unreal in a way her whole life had been spent out of control in the blink of an eye. Fuck it, she thought. All she could do was roll with the punches at this point.

Vida felt the bar and leaned against the wall facing the stage as Young Buck came out. The New York crowd roared, showing Young Buck love. Vida was unmoved. In a pair of skin-tight Seven jeans, a short sleeve Prada shirt, and Prada boots, she looked like she was trying to pick up a man. Out the corner of her eye she saw a smooth brown-skinned dude coming her way. Vida sighed slightly, she didn't want to be bothered.

As the dude got closer, she could see that the dude was attractive, but that made no difference—her mood was not going to change.

Pulling up on Vida, the dude said, "What's up, ma?" His gear and jewels made him look like a rap star.

"Ain't shit." Vida said flatly, with her arms folded across her chest. She looked the dude up and down like he was holding her up.

Picking up on Vida's attitude the dude said, "Damn, sexy, who pissed you off tonight? Show 'em to me and I'll deal wit' they ass, that's my word, ma."

Vida cracked a slight smile. The dude was funny, in a bamma way.

With a bright smile and a smooth nod, the dude said, "Okay, I got you smilin', I'm gettin' somewhere...you look so much sexier when you smile."

"Thank you." Vida's smile went away and she was serious once again, she wanted to send the dude on his way before Tia returned.

"You alone, ma?" The dude asked, checking out Vida's sexy body.

"Nah. I'm here wit' my girlfriend, but we ain't gon' be here that long. I really don't feel good."

"Damn, I wanted to take you up to VIP for a few drinks." The bamma said. Vida was unmoved. "Come on, ma, let me take you up to VIP. You can kick back and enjoy the show from there. You'll feel better. You smoke?"

Vida thought about the VIP offer for a second. However, Tonio already had a man inside the club that was going to get her and Tia in the VIP section so she didn't need this stranger for that. Getting straight to the point, Vida said, "Look, you seem like a nice dude, but I don't know you and I don't hang out wit' strangers, boo. Sorry."

The dude smirked arrogantly. "You ain't from New York, are you?"

"Why?" Vida rolled her eyes.

"Cause if you was from New York, I'm sure you'd know who I am."

Vida laughed. "Is that right?"

"Yeah, my name is Manny." He extended his hand. Vida shook it. "What's your name, sexy?"

"Vickie," Vida responded quickly on her toes.

"Well, now we know each other, can I take you up to the VIP section now?"

Vida smiled, even though the nigga was getting on her nerves. "I gotta pass on that, boo. Maybe I'll see you around later." She winked at him.

The club exploded with cheers, it somewhat caught Vida off guard. 50 Cent was now on the stage. He went straight into, "In Da Club", sending the crowd into a frenzy.

Looking over his shoulder at 50 Cent, Manny rubbed his chin and looked back at Vida. "You broke my heart that fast, ma. I hope I do see you later." Without another word, Manny disappeared into the thick crowd.

Moments later, Tia was back on the scene. "Who was that bamma you was talkin' to, Vee?"

"Some nigga name Manny, he wanted to take me up to VIP but I brushed him off."

"Oh yeah?" Tia used the darkness of the club to discretely slide Vida a compact Ruger .45 automatic.

Smoothly, Vida slipped the pistol inside her Gucci handbag.

"What's up wit' the dude that's supposed to get us in VIP?"

The 50 Cent performance had the walls of the club shaking, and the crowd was going off.

"Whoever it is should meet us by the bar in a few minutes." Tia said, looking around the club. "I just got a text

tellin' me to be on point. Everything is in motion, boo."
She winked at Vida. "You ready, Vee?"

"Always, you know that. I just want to get the shit
over and done wit'."

Tia rubbed Vida's shoulder. "I feel you, boo. I know
how you feel. All this shit gon' be behind us in a minute
and we gon' be able to start all over."

Vida sighed. "I don't know about that, Tee...All this
might be behind us, but we ain't gon' never be able to really start over. We done lost too much. The most we can
do is move on and put this behind us as best as we can."

Tia nodded. "You right, Vee." She shrugged. "We
gotta keep it movin' though." Tia was doing her best to
block everything out of her mind. The higher she was the
less stressed she felt.

Out of the blue, Tia changed the subject and said,
"Damn, he sexy as shit, I'd love to fuck him."

"Who?" Vida looked around the club.

"50, girl. Look at that nigga wit' his shirt off."

Vida sucked her teeth and gave up a look like, *please!*
"You trippin' like shit...I don't even like that bamma, he
talk too much shit. You know real niggas don't do that
where we come from, plus, he be doin' all that hot-ass
name callin'."

Tia laughed, nodding her head to the song. "You got a
point but when you doin' it big you can talk big shit."

"Yeah, I guess so." Vida said uninterested in talking
about 50 Cent.

Moments later, a beautiful model-like woman walked
up on Vida and Tia and said, "I'm Tonio's friend. Come
wit' me."

Vida and Tia gave each other quick glances and then followed the beautiful woman through the thick crowd.

Once in the VIP section, Tonio's beautiful industry contact got Vida and Tia a personal booth, a few bottles of Patron, and put them on point about who was who. Now Vida and Tia knew exactly who Romel, Manny and their hired guns were. Vida couldn't believe that Manny had walked straight into her hands and she had brushed him off. After Vida and Tia were comfortable and didn't look out of place, Tonio's beautiful industry contact made her way out of the club.

Slowly sipping her glass of Patron, Vida had her eyes on Manny and Romel as they mixed in with everybody that was supposed to be somebody. It was clear that Manny and Romel were heavyweights. Looking at Tia, Vida said, "As soon as the dude Manny see me he gon' be all over me again, watch."

Rockin' a slick-ass pair of Prada shades, Tia has her eyes on Manny and Romel as well.

"That might be our move right there, Vee. If the nigga come over here sweatin' you, we gon' use his ass to smoke the nigga Romel and it's a wrap."

"Cool." Vida said. The Patron was calming her nerves and it was very much needed. She was even nodding her head to 50 Cent's, "21 Questions".

Tia took another good look at Manny and said, "The bamma Manny jive look like Kobe Bryant."

"Yeah, a little bit." Vida took another sip from her glass.

Killing the last of her drink, Tia stood up and said, "Let me walk around for a second, I might be able to get Romel's attention. If you can get the nigga Manny's attention work your magic."

"I got you." Vida gave Tia a wink.

Tia stepped off swinging her ass with attitude. It wouldn't be hard to get Romel's attention with an ass and a walk like hers.

Seeing Vida's sexy ass alone, dudes were all over her no sooner than Tia stepped off. Politely but firmly, she was shooting them down as quickly as they were coming. That is until the man of the hour pulled up.

"How you doin', ma?" Romel towered over Vida holding a drink in his hand.

Vida looked up at him and said, "I'm good, just waitin' for my friend to come back." Vida couldn't believe her luck. Manny and Romel had both tried to holla at her in the same night.

"Is that right? You here wit' a dude? I don't recall seein' you wit' a dude earlier." Romel smiled.

"Nah, I ain't wit' a dude, I'm wit' my girl. She stepped off for a second, but she'll be right back."

"You talkin' 'bout that light-skinned shortie I saw you wit'?"

Vida felt uncomfortable that Romel was already paying close attention to her and Tia.

"Yeah, that's my girl." Vida smiled.

"Is that your girl, like your lover, or like your homegirl?"

Vida gave him a look that read: What the fuck?!

"No offense, ma but nowadays a nigga gotta ask, not that I got a problem wit' it."

Romel smiled, running a hand over his smooth, wavy hair. The diamonds in his watch and ring glistened all over the VIP section.

"Nah, that ain't my thing there." Vida sipped her drink.

Glancing around the VIP section, Romel sipped his drink and said, "I hate to see you sittin' over here alone, you too gorgeous for that."

Vida pretended to blush, and wondered how the whole situation would play out. As cold-hearted as she felt, she could smoke Romel and never think about it again.

"Can I have a seat, I'd love to keep you company for a minute?" Romel nodded at the spot right beside Vida.

"I been shootin' niggas down all night. It's gon' be a lot of haters if I give you some play." Vida smiled.

"Fuck the haters. Let me worry 'bout that, ma."

Vida shrugged. "Cool, have a seat then."

"So what's your name?" Romel sat right beside Vida and put an arm around her.

"Vickie." Vida wasn't feeling the arm around her, but she didn't trip.

"Where you from?"

"Maryland." Vida smiled. "What's your name?"

Romel gave Vida a sexy smirk. "Come on, ma, you gotta know my name. I don't think nobody up in here don't know my name. This my club."

"My bad." Vida smiled. "This your club for real?" She pretended to be impressed.

Romel laughed, he was feeling Vida.

"Yeah, it's my club, ma. My name' Romel...Ask around about me."

Vida smiled. This nigga is real on hisself, she thought.

"Okay, big daddy, I'm on point now."

Smiling, Romel said, "So what part of Maryland you from? I got peoples down there in Baltimore and D.C."

Vida didn't feel comfortable with Romel asking so many questions.

"I'm from Rockville, you know people in Rockville?" She wanted to be the one asking the questions.

"Nah, but I been shoppin' down there." Romel joked. "So what brings you out tonight, you a 50 Cent fan?"

"Not really, he cool, but me and my girl just wanted to hit the club since we were in New York."

"You and your girl know how to pull strings to be able to get up in VIP."

Vida shrugged with a smile. "What can I say...When you look good you end up in VIP."

Romel found that funny. "Yeah, that's how it goes, ain't it?" He took a good look at Vida, finding her so sexy. She had him turned on from the moment he laid eyes on her.

"You do look good, ma. If it was up to me you'd be in more than VIP."

"Is that right?" Vida acted impressed.

Romel began to lay it on thick. Vida went with the program, making Romel believe she was really feeling him.

Manny pulled up on the scene while Romel was laying his rap game down. For real, for real, Manny was fucked up when he saw Vida smiling and laughing with Romel after she had brushed him off earlier. But, he played it cool.

"Damn. Ma, we meet again, but my man got your ear."

Vida shrugged with a smile, even though she wasn't feeling Romel or Manny. "What can I say...sittin' alone makes me look like I need company."

With his arm still around Vida, Romel looked at Manny and said, "You know Vickie?"

"Not really, I ran into her downstairs, we shared a few words, but she wouldn't give me any play." Manny said.

Vida gave him a serious look and said, "I told you I wasn't feelin' well."

Before anyone could say another word, Tia stepped on the scene.

"Damn, Vee, you got a lot of company don't you?"

Romel and Manny took a good look at Tia and were impressed by her sex appeal.

Vida said, "This is my girl, Tammy." Looking Tia up and down, undressing her with his eyes, Manny said, "How nice to meet you, sexy." He extended his hand.

Tia shook Manny's hand. "Nice to meet you as well." She smiled.

Romel extended his free hand to Tia as she shook it he said, "What's good, ma? I'm Romel and that's my right-hand man, Manny."

With a lustful smile, Manny looked from Vida to Tia and said, "Now it's two on two, we can have our own private party."

Tia winked at Manny, like she was in accord with all of his thoughts.

"Sounds good to me, I'm always down for a good time, but it's up to my girl." She nodded toward Vida.

Romel looked at Vida and smoothly said, "You down, ma?"

Vida nodded with a smile and said, "Yeah, I'm down. I need to have a little fun."

Manny said, "Let me get us some bottles.

"Hold up," Romel got up. "Manny, let me holla at you 'bout somethin' real quick." Romel looked back at Vida and Tia and said, "We'll be right back ladies, don't go nowhere." He smiled.

"We gon' be right here." Tia said.

Romel and Manny stepped off and headed for the bar.

Tia looked at Vida once they were alone and said, "You catchin' big tonight, ain't you?"

Unmoved, Vida said, "I guess so...I wish we could just smoke these niggas right here and get the fuck on 'bout our business."

"I feel you." Tia smoothly pulled out the cell phone Tonio had given her and sent him a text message saying: *We got the nigga right where we want him. I told you I got you, nigga.*

Tonio hit right back: *I knew it, keep me on point, ma.*

Tia put the phone up. Looking at Vida, she said, "Let's get these niggas to take us to a hotel."

Sipping the last of her drink, Vida said "Fuck it, let's take care of this shit."

Ecstasy

Driver sucked Lala's hard nipple as his hands rubbed all over her naked body.

Rolling off two "E" pills, Lala moaned, "I'm so wet, Driver. Ahhh...Yeah, I been thinkin' 'bout you fuckin' me all day."

Driver and Lala were alone in Lala's bedroom. They'd made time to get away from the drama to hook up for another session of thug lovin'. They were both naked with the covers pulled back.

Lil Wayne was still playing in the CD player, but he wasn't killing the mood. Nothing could kill the mood when Driver and Lala got together, especially when they were off the "E" pills.

He licked and sucked her nipples and squeezed her breasts like he was much older than 16, he knew how to please Lala.

Looking up into Lala's eyes, Driver whispered, "You smell so good." He continued to make love to her breast. He slid a hand between her legs and slipped a finger inside her, making her moan again, nice and long. He was pleasing her. His every touch made her feel as if she was about to cum. The "E" had him feeling like a pro, he was on top of his shit. It was all about pleasing her.

133

He was turned on by how wet and warm she was.

"You wet as shit."

"Ahh... I know...Ssss. I know." She felt her orgasm coming on fast and hard and Driver hadn't even dug inside her with his erection yet.

He was enjoying teasing her, playing with her pussy lips and rubbing and squeezing her clit. In and out of her pussy he stroked with his middle finger. It felt so good to Lala and her moans confirmed it.

"Oh yeah, Driver." She moaned as he slipped a second finger inside her. She couldn't stop moaning and grinding against the motions of his fingers.

"Taste my pussy, boo." She panted. "Suck my pussy like you did last time, Driver."

He smirked. "I got you." With smoothness, he made his way down to her wet pussy.

"Sssss...Yeah, boo." She hissed and moaned as soon as his tongue got to her clit.

"You like it?" Driver managed to say in between licks.

"Yeah, boo, oh God, yeah." She rubbed the back of his head with her soft hands.

Driver worked her with his tongue until she was begging for him to fuck her.

Smoothly, he grabbed a condom off the nightstand, tore it open with his teeth, and slid on the protection. Wasting no time, he climbed on top of her and slid inside her tight wetness, nice and slow. He kissed her, sucked her tongue and sucked her neck.

Lala wrapped her legs around Driver and used them to pull him deeper inside her pussy as he stroked her long and slow, just as she liked to be fucked. She moaned slow and deep like he was killing her slowly.

His strokes got stronger and faster. Her leg lock helped him to fuck her at the pace she wanted.

The headboard began to bang against the wall with force.

With every stroke, as they got harder and deeper, Lala cringed. Driver dug deeper and harder and faster into her tight, wet pussy when he saw her cringe. He knew he was fucking the shit out of her.

"Fuck me from the back!" she shouted.

Driver got her on her hands and knees in a flash and dug right back inside her tightness. He gripped her small waist and began fucking her roughly, making her moan loudly.

"Smack my ass, boo." She shouted. "Sssss. Oh yeah, do it again, ow, ow, ow…"

He continued to smack her ass and make her moan.

Minutes on the clock began to fly as they fucked nice and hard rolling off the pills. They were drenched with sweat.

Fucking her hard and fast, making her moan as if she were on fire, Driver's hands found ways to squeeze her ass, rub her breasts and pinch her nipples. It made her cum.

"Oh shit!" she shouted, fucking him back. "I'm cummin', I'm cummin', I'm cummin'!" She screamed it over and over.

Everything inside of Driver tingled. He could feel his nut coming. He put his all in his pounding strokes. He stroked her, making her scream like he was killing her.

135

She continued to throw it back, fucking him back like she was fighting back.

"That's right, Lala, fuck me back, girl." He shouted, holding her waist with her head back, his eyes closed. He was racing to the finish line now.

He was killing the pussy one stroke at a time and Lala made sounds as if it was the best fucking in the world.

"Ummmhmmmm." She moaned. She could feel another orgasm coming. Damn, this young nigga is killing me, she thought.

Driver grunted, ready to cum. He needed to cum. It made him fuck her harder.

"Uh, uh, uh…" she couldn't take it anymore. He loved the fact that he was in control and was punishing the pussy now. He was satisfied now.

"You are fuckin' the shit out…Of…Me!" Lala felt him deep inside her stomach. Filled with satisfaction.

Her moans and grunts stroked his ego and made the fuck feel so good.

She came again, so hard that she began to shake and feel faint. "I can't believe you got me cummin' again." She moaned. "Ahhh, don't stop, don't stop, I'm cummin' so hard this time."

Driver smiled and let his nut go like a shotgun blast. "Uuunnngh…Damn, girl." He grunted. He tensed and pumped into her with a strong force. He moaned, panted, groaned, whatever he could do to get his nut out. He came hard and thick inside the condom. Slowing his strokes down as he got the last of his load out, he said, "I want my name on this pussy."

Out of breath, Lala tried to laugh. "You ain't ready to put your name on this pussy."

"Shit, try me." He said, slowly stroking her.

Driver and Lala took a hot shower together and fucked real good one more time. They couldn't get enough of one another.

After their shower they got dressed in Lala's bedroom and put another Backwood in the air.

Holding the purple haze in his lungs as he passed Lala the Backwood, Driver said, "See y'all on some real live gun play wit' them Most Wanted bitches, huh?" He checked the clip of his .40 Ruger and slid it between his waistband.

Lala shook her head as she took a pull of the Backwood.

"Paris trippin' like shit. She think she Vida or Tia or some shit...I really ain't wit' all that bullshit for real." Lala went on to tell Driver about everything that had gone down earlier with Most Wanted, all the way up to the shooting.

Driver laughed.

"Y'all better slow the fuck down. You see how Vida and Tia all over the news and shit." He stood up, ready to hit the streets again.

"Yeah, I know." Lala shook her head and passed the Backwood back to Driver.

He took a long pull and handed it back to her.

"Kill it, boo. I gotta run." He kissed her forehead. "I'll catch up wit' you tomorrow."

"We gon' pick up where we left off?" She smiled.

"You know it." Driver headed for the door.

Driver left Lala's apartment and hit the block. Saratoga Avenue was pumpin', but nobody seemed to be on the block so Driver was makin' a killin' getting all the sells.

Mechanic walked up and said, "Aye, Driver, do somethin' wit' me for seventy-five."

"I got you." Driver led Mechanic inside the building and served him for 20 rocks.

Mechanic stuffed the coke inside the pockets of his shorts.

"Where everybody at?"

"Counting his money", Driver said, "I don't know, moe. Niggas might be at the go-go, that's where I'm bout to go soon as I make another few hundred."

Mechanic gave Driver a pound. "Catch you later, shorty." He headed down the hallway.

Driver stepped back outside and made a quick three hundred dollars in no time. His crew hit his cell phone, one after the other, and told him to meet them at the "Mad Chef" club, where Backyard Band was on stage doing their thing. Wasting no time, Driver jumped in his car and headed for the go-go.

Inside his Impala SS with Lil Wayne's "Bring it Back" off Tha Carter CD, blasting through the speakers,

Driver cruised down Benning Road with his .40 caliber on his lap. There were only a few cars in front of him as he pulled up at the stoplight.

However, one car behind driver's Impala was Styles and Eric in a dark-gray Monte Carlo with tinted windows. They had been following Driver for several blocks.

Puting on his ski mask, riding shotgun, Styles said, "I'ma smoke this nigga right here at the light."

Looking around to make sure they could get away with the murder, Eric said, "Hurry up, moe, get on top of it and let's get out of here."

Gripping a huge chrome .50 Caliber Desert Eagles that could stop a rhino in its tracks, Styles quickly got out of the car. Death was in the air. There was no way Styles was going to let Driver get away with disrespecting him.

Swiftly, Styles walked up on the back of Driver's car, ready to open fire, but he wanted a clear shot.

Driver saw movement in his rear view. The ski mask grabbed his attention. "Shit!" he shouted, jumping out of the car with his .40 cal. Blasting.

The shots flew by Styles' head, making him duck, but he let the Desert Eagle go at the same time. The gun sounded off like a two thousand pound bomb dropped over Baghdad.

The powerful slug from the Desert Eagle slammed into Driver's chest with the force of a flying 747 and knocked him to the ground. Styles ran around the car and let shorty have it five more times in the face with the .50. It was a sight like no other!

Cars at the light smashed the gas and got the fuck out of dodge.

Smoking Desert Eagle in hand, Styles looked down at the destruction of the .50 and decided to pick up Driver's Ruger. He then ran back to the car and jumped in.

Stomping the gas to get them out of the area, Eric said, "Damn, moe, you punished that nigga!" He sounded excited.

"Yeah, I know it's fucked up I had to punish shorty like that but he jumped out there." Styles looked over his shoulder to make sure no one was on their back.

Looking at the Ruger that Styles had taken from Driver, Eric laughed and said, "Damn, you took his hamma, too. Let me see that joint."

Styles passed Eric the pistol.

"This muhfucka pretty as shit." Eric checked the pistol out as he hit all back streets of the south side of town. "Let me get this joint, moe."

Styles shook his head with a smirk on his face. "You can have it, shorty."

"Good lookin' out." Eric said. He loved Rugers.

A short while later, the go-go band, Backyard, was crankin' like shit. They were hitting a go-go version of Three 6 Mafia's, "Stay Fly". The crowd was feeling the song.

The honeys in the spot were looking phat-to-death-and off the "E" pills feeling real good and sexy.

For the moment there was no tension in the air amongst the dudes or the girl crews. But, the night was still young.

The club was called, The Mad Chef, it was a short ride outside of D.C. in PG County, Maryland.

Changing the pace, Backyard's front man, 'Big G', started working the crowd, acknowledging the different hoods and crews that were in the spot. Pointing toward the First and Kennedy street crew, 'Big G' shouted into the mic, "I see you KDY! Throw ya guns in the air!"

Every word 'Big G' shouted was in harmony with the go-go beat. "Oy Boys, I see you!"

He pointed at the Barry Farms niggas. One by one, 'Big G' got everybody, 57th niggas, Simple City niggas, Forrest Creek, Homer Ave, Benning Park, and a few others.

Feeling left out, the Most Wanted Honies made it known they were in the spot. They waved their hands in the air for 'Big G' to get them. He did.

"Most Wanted!" 'Big G' shouted, winking at Summer's sexy-ass. Most Wanted had to be close to fifty deep. "Who the fuck want it wit' the Most Wanted!"

Most Wanted was pleased.

'Big G' spotted the other girl crews and showed them all love: The KO Honeys, the X-Rated Honeys and the Survivor Honeys. All the girl crews were deep as shit, like little armies.

High as shit off the smoke and the pill, with a little Remy in their system as well, Lil Rose and his man Marky, were just coming through the door with a few of their Saratoga avenue homies. Right behind them, The

Fuck'em Up Honeys came through the door damn near thirty deep. Their name fit them well.

Feeling on top of his game, Lil Rose saw a bad ass X-Rated Honey that he knew and grabbed her from behind, wrapping his hands around her waist. She looked over her shoulder and smiled when she saw it was Lil Rose. He winked at her, grinding against her soft, round ass to the go-go beat. It made him hard instantly. She grinded her ass back against him even harder when she felt how stiff he was getting.

Looking over her shoulder at Lil Rose again, she shouted, "You feel like you want some of this pussy!"

Lil Rose smiled. "We can leave together tonight!"

'Big G' spotted Lil Rose and shouted into the mic, "I see you, Lil Rose! You and them Toga Boys...Them Toga Boys ain't goin' for shit!"

Lil Rose heard his name and put his hand in the air. He smiled and nodded at 'Big G' who was only a few feet away from him.

'Big G' and Backyard kept it moving and went into their go-go version of Cassidy's hit song, "I'm a Hustla". Working the crowd, 'Big G' kept shouting the hook of the song. "I'ma hustla...I'ma, I'ma hustla!"

A short while later, 'Big G' saw Styles, Eric and a few Congress Park niggas that fucked with Eric. 'Big G' got right on top of acknowledging Styles and crew.

"Congress Park, don't be so mean! I see you, Styles!"

Styles nodded his head at 'Big G'. Every time Styles stepped in the go-go whoever was on the mic always showed him love.

Driver's murder wasn't even an hour old yet and Styles was out and about like it wasn't shit to it.

When Lil Rose heard Styles' name he looked around until he spotted him. Lil Rose really didn't like how shit had gone down earlier between Driver and Styles. He wanted to holla at Styles and see if he could smooth things out. After all, Driver was a youngin', he really didn't know any better, Lil Rose thought. He made his way through the crowd so he could pull up on Styles.

Pulling up on Styles, Lil Rose shouted, "Styles, let me holla at you, moe!"

Styles gave Lil Rose a funny look. Lil Rose had surprised him and appeared out of nowhere. However, Styles played it real cool. "What's good, Lil Rose?"

Eric mean-mugged Lil Rose from the side.

Lil Rose caught Eric's look but acted like he didn't. "I need to holla at you real quick, alone."

Flatly, Styles said, "I ain't got no rap, shorty."

Lil Rose frowned up his face. He was fucked up and felt disrespected.

"Oh yeah, it's like that, now?"

"Yeah." Styles nodded with a cold look in his eyes. "It's like that."

Lil Rose mugged on Styles, Eric and the rest of the niggas with them.

"Cool." he stepped off. Bitch ass niggas got me fucked up, Lil Rose thought.

Moments later, 'Big G' and Backyard were still doing their thing, crankin' like shit. 'Big G' saw a few latecomers and pointed their way, showing love. "I see my man, Cinquan, and the Real Live crew. What's up, keep it Real Live."

Cinquan and his Real Live entourage came through like they owned the place. Their movement was strong in the D.C. streets. The rap game was only the beginning for the Real Live family.

'Big G' nodded at his man scoop who was right beside Cinquan, they were both killin' 'em in Gucci gear.

"Scoop, I see you, slim. It's a Real Live thing. I feel you, slim. Death before dishonor." 'Big G' continued to shout out.

The go-go band kept it moving. 'Big G' had Backyard hitting everything the crowd wanted to hear. He spotted another crew and showed them love.

"Aw shit! I see them Hell Razor Honeys!"

The Hell Razor Honeys came through the door a good twenty strong. They looked like they were on a mission. Tension hit the air like tear gas. Everyone could feel it.

Hearing that the Hell Razor Honeys were in the spot, the Most Wanted Honeys knew it was on. They were ready, plus they had the X-Rated Honeys with them. Surely, the Hell Razor Honeys were outnumbered.

Without talking, the Hell Razor Honeys, led by a sexy 20 year old honey by the name of Shontae, charged Most Wanted. All hell broke loose with an explosion of violence. The music stopped. People scattered as the girls clashed like warring infantry troops. Blood hit the floor fast. Hell Razor had razors and box cutters, some had knives. Five huge security guards rushed the scene, trying to establish control. It was no use. Shit was way too live and out of control.

X-Rated joined the fight, helping Most Wanted. Although Hell Razor was cutting bitches something serious, it looked like Most Wanted and X-Rated were getting the best of the fight. That changed quickly when the Fuck'em Up Honeys joined Hell Razor and took the commotion to a whole new level. There was no way security was going to be able to gain control without the help of PG County Police.

Shontae had a Most Wanted honey against the wall pounding her with blows from her fist and a box cutter. The box cutter was doing major damage to the girl's pretty face. The girl fought back hard but Shontae was too much for her. Seconds later, the girl hit the floor hard and fast, covering her bleeding face. She screamed in pain as Shontae stomped and kicked her in the head.

"Dirty-ass bitch!" Shontae shouted. Her victim would be blessed if she woke up in a hospital, only pissing blood with countless stitches in her lacerated face and nothing more.

Right behind Shontae, six Fuck'em Up Honeys were all over a security guard like pit bulls, stabbing the shit out of him.

Eric saw two Hell Razor Honeys beating the shit out of his baby's mother, a Most Wanted Honey. Eric rushed the girls, grabbed one by the hair and knocked her slam out with a crushing left hook. It was a heavy weight punch that broke her jaw. Two Hell Razor Honeys attacked him swinging box cutters. One opened a deep slice across his face before he knocked her out cold. Three more Hell Razor Honeys rushed him with box cutters followed by a gang of Fuck 'em Up Honeys. In seconds, Eric was trying to find the door with his face and arms sliced and bloody.

PG County Police rushed inside the club spraying mace and swinging nightsticks, forcing everyone out the door. They grabbed a lot of girls and arrested them on the spot.

Outside of, The Mad Chef, PG County Police cars with flashing lights were all over the place. Officers were rushing anyone that wasn't moving fast enough. People were running in every direction, it was like a riot. Groups of girls were still fighting in the parking lot.

A few Hell Razor Honeys were trying to make a run for it across Central Avenue to their car. Out of the blue, automatic gunfire tore through the air. A bloody Eric was blasting a .40 caliber Ruger at the girls. He dropped one right in the middle of Central Avenue. PG County Police wasted no time, they opened fire on Eric. He spun around in a bloody rage and shot off at PG, he didn't stand a chance. PG cut him down with countless bullets. Eric's lifeless body fell dead with Driver's pistol in hand.

In the parking lot on the other side of Central Avenue, crowds of people were still running for their cars. The gunfire had panic setting in.

Paris, Tera, and Lala were inside Mechanic's Impala in the back of the dark parking lot watching all of the drama. Paris was behind it all, she'd sent Shontae and the rest of the Hell Razor Honeys inside the club to attack Most Wanted. She wanted everybody to rush outside in a state of panic.

Sitting in the back seat of the Impala, Paris said to Tera, "Start the car up, T."

All three girls were nervous after hearing all the gunfire. From their position they couldn't see Eric's shooting, but they knew somebody was getting busy with that heat. As far as Paris was concerned, the gunfire was the perfect cover for what she had in mind.

Shaken up by the gunfire, Lala looked back at Paris from the passenger's seat and said, "It's too many police out here, Paris. Let's get the fuck outta here."

Irritated, Paris sucked her teeth and said, "Fuck that shit!" On her lap was a black 9mm Beretta with a long silencer on it. Lil Rose let her use the gun. "Them bitches wanna get into some gunplay shit, we gon' give they ass the muhfuckin' business."

Tera spotted Summer and a few other Most Wanted Honies running to their car.

"There go them bitches right there." She pointed at the group of girls.

Lala felt her heart skip a beat. She wanted no parts of murder.

Paris cocked the hammer of the Beretta without a second thought. "I got these bitches." She got out the car, aimed at Summer, and fired. Slugs hit Summer in the chest. Her girls screamed and ran in all directions as

Summer's body hit the ground. Paris fired ten more silenced shots and then jumped back in the car. She smacked the back of Tera's seat and shouted, "Let's get the fuck outta here!"

Tera pulled off and drove right past Summer's body as they pulled into traffic on Central Avenue. Cars were flying in all directions trying to get away from the violence.

Lala got a good look a Summer's body laying on the ground bleeding with bullet wounds to the chest. The sight turned her stomach. She began to think that Paris had lost her mind.

Smoking pistol in hand, Paris said, "That'll hold her bad-ass." She smiled wickedly.

Mission Complete

Weed smoke filled the New Jersey motel room that Romel had gotten for the night. He couldn't wait to slide inside Vida's pussy. Everything about her turned him on, all the way down to her sexy Dolce and Gabbana fragrance. Romel sat on the bed with his arm around Vida, licking her ear.

"You smell so good, ma...so sexy. Mmmm." Romel whispered.

Vida flashed a fake smile, but on the real Romel's words turned her stomach. His breath smelled like hard liquor, cigarettes, and weed smoke. He had to be crazy if he thought he was getting some pussy. Blowing weed smoke in the air, Vida said, "You feelin' me, huh, big boy?"

"By all means." He licked the side of her face.

Vida glanced at Romel's 9mm that was lying on the nightstand. It was in arms reach. She was wondering how she and Tia were going to get the jump on Romel and Manny.

Across from Vida and Romel, on the other bed, Manny was all over Tia, hugging her and kissing on her. His .40 caliber was still in his shoulder holster in full view.

Rubbing Tia's breasts, Manny said, "Ma, you got me hard as shit."

Tia rubbed between his legs. His jeans couldn't hide what he was working with.

"Mmmm, I see. You jive workin' wit' somethin', too." She smiled. Although she was thinking about blowing Manny's brains out, his hands all over her were feeling good being as though she was still rolling off the "E" pill.

Rubbing his hand between Tia's legs, Manny whispered, "Wait 'til I get inside that pussy."

Tia laughed. Man, you got another thing coming, she thought. Passing the burning Dutch back to Manny, she said, "Let me use the bathroom real quick." She took her purse with her and shot Vida a look like: Let's handle this business. Vida's body language let it be known that she was ready.

Romel's cell phone went off with a Jay-Z ring tone. He took his arm from around Vida and answered the phone. "What's up, Mal?" He went on to have a quick conversation about business.

Tia stepped out of the bathroom with her .45 in both hands.

"Get off the fuckin' phone!" she hissed, aiming at Romel's head.

At the same time, in a flash Vida pulled her .45 and jumped to her feet aiming at Manny's head as she stepped away from the bed.

Manny smiled. "Get the fuck outta here." He was smart enough not to move.

Slowly, Romel ended the call and dropped the phone on the floor.

"What's up wit' this shit, ma?" he asked, not believing two badass honeys got the jump on him.

Looking at Manny with a serious look in her eyes, Vida said, "Get the fuck on the floor, and move slow, nigga."

Tia winked at Romel and said, "You, too. Get on the floor. Face down!"

Manny and Romel slowly eased to the floor, angered and uncertain.

Swiftly, Tia snatched Manny's pistol out of the holster and tossed it to Vida. She then grabbed Romel's off the nightstand. Now they had two pistols pointed at Romel and Manny.

Pissed off, Romel said, "What the fuck is this all about?"

Manny looked up at Vida and Tia and said, "You bitches must be crazy as-"

Tia kicked him in the face and shut him up.

"Bitch-ass nigga, you must be crazy!" She cocked the hammer of the .45. "Watch your mouth!"

Manny grunted in pain and grabbed his bleeding mouth.

Romel saw that the girls were serious. "What do you want?" he asked, trying to reason with Tia.

Ready to get the shit over with, Vida shot Romel in the head with two quick shots that shook the room. Tia jumped, the loud pops caught her off guard.

Manny knew it was all or nothing once Vida smoked Romel. He tried to get up to rush Tia since she was close to him.

Boom! Boom! Boom! Boom!

Tia didn't think twice. She pumped Manny full of lead from two pistols before he even made it to his feet. His bloody body slumped to the floor, lifelessly.

Looking at Vida, Tia said, "Grab their car keys. Our work is done here."

Vida stepped over Romel's bloody body and grabbed the keys to his Benz.

A Day in Court

"**G**overnment had no case!" was the headline that the *Los Angeles Times* printed after sources gave a reporter information that all government witnesses against No Draws could no longer remember "anything" when it came time to go in front of the grand jury. There would be no indictment, for sure.

On a legal visit with her lawyer, No Draws had a smile on her face that just wouldn't go away. She was sure she'd be a free woman once again, very soon. She would be back on top of her game no sooner than she hit the streets.

In his smooth voice, her lawyer Lawrence said, "I don't know what you did, but everyone seems to forget, or better yet, they forgot what they told detectives."

No Draws smiled brighter. With a shrug, she said, "What can I say, you can't hold a good bitch down."

Flipping through some papers, Lawrence said, "Tell me how you did it, Shelly. What did you do?"

"Nothing, I didn't do anything, Lawrence."

"Come on now, I'm your lawyer, you can talk to me."

No Draws leaned across the table and kissed Lawrence on the lips. She licked his lips and then bit his bottom lip.

"Some things you take to the grave wit' you. You know that, boo." She smiled and leaned back in her seat.

Lawrence licked his lips and smiled. He felt his erection growing between his legs. No Draws had that kind of affect on most men. Lawrence was no exception to the rule, being a married man didn't make him off limits to No Draws.

"Shelly, you are one of a kind, you know that?"

She smiled and winked at him. "I'm glad you think so. So when do I get out of this bitch?"

"Everything should be done in a day or so, no more than a week, and you're free to go."

In a sexy voice, she said, "I'm going to show you a good time when I get out. You know that, right?"

"Yeah, I look forward to that." Lawrence said. His mind drifted back to the first time he was with No Draws sexually.

A number of Hollywood big shots were at the home of Bruce Dickerson, a heavyweight movie producer. Dickerson had just given No Draws the lead role in his upcoming movie, "East Side Love", and he was throwing a party to celebrate his new joint venture with HBO.

As always, No Draws was in the spot meeting new people and networking hard. She had a few movies under her belt by this time so she was feeling herself.

Looking like new money, No Draws made her way through the crowded living room in a black Prada dress that showed off her sexy body. Everyone knew who she was and that turned her on and made her feel powerful. Producers, filmmakers, actors and more were all laughing and joking talking that "Hollywood talk."

No Draws saw Lawrence and his wife across the room talking to Bruce Dickerson. She made eye contact with Lawrence and felt a connection. Something about him made her wet. The fact that he was with his wife made her want him even more. He was a taken man. That was a turn on for No Draws.

After talking to a few people as she made her way through the crowd, No Draws bumped into Lawrence alone as she headed to the bathroom.

He smiled. "Shelly, how are you doing?"

"Good, real good." She said as she checked him out. He was in a finely pressed Gucci suit and a Gucci shirt with no tie, looking so good.

"I saw you with your wife so I didn't really want to rush over and make a scene."

He smiled. "I understand. I hear you got the lead role in, "East Side Love". That's a good look."

"Thank you."

Looking around to make sure no one was paying them any attention, Lawrence said, "I saw how you looked at me. I felt that connection, Shelly. I noticed it the last time we ran into each other at Liz's."

No Draws shook her head with a smile. "Trust me, Lawrence, you don't want to do this."

"Why not?"

"I'll have you leaving your wife."

Lawrence grabbed her face, softly, with his hand and kissed her. His tongue explored her mouth. It felt so wrong, but so good at the same time.

"I want to make love to you, Shelly."

Soaking wet between the legs, No Draws said, "Meet me upstairs in five minutes."

Five minutes later No Draws and Lawrence were alone in a plush bedroom with the door locked. Hugging and kissing like old lovers, they stood in the middle of the room, breathing hard. Both extremely aroused. Lawrence's touch made No Draws want to please, want to fuck him, want to suck the life out of him while his wife was downstairs, most likely looking for him.

He squeezed her breasts. "Take this off." He commanded.

She moaned from his touch as he undressed her. When she stood before him naked he understood why men chased her around Hollywood. Her body was outstanding.

"You are beautiful, Shelly. So damn beautiful."

No Draws saw his erection trying to force its way through his pants. She grabbed it, he moaned and his manhood was so hard it hurt. He began to undress with speed, as if his clothes were on fire.

Naked, he grabbed her and kissed her deeply, running his hands through her hair. He led her to the bed and laid her down. She felt the fire between her legs burning out of control as she found herself lying on a luxurious bed in an enormous house in the Hollywood Hills.

Lawrence got on top of her and kissed her with intense passion. She loved the way he felt on top of her. His kisses went to her breasts. She moaned and rubbed his back. His kisses made their way to her nipples making them stand firm and tall. She closed her eyes and arched her back in serious ecstasy as she wrapped her legs around him. The wetness between her legs could put out a fire.

Lawrence whispered, "You are so sexy, Shelly…Ahh…" His kisses moved lower and he licked down her stomach, and made her squirm and moan as if she was dying for him to slide inside her.

Rubbing his head, she said, "You got me so damn wet." She eased his head down toward her dripping pussy.

He ran his tongue over her clit and bit it lightly, making her moan loudly. She shivered and pushed her pussy up into his face. It wouldn't take much more to make her cum. It was building up with every passing second of pleasure.

Moaning from deep within, No Draws said, "Oh God, ssssss…don't stop…Please don't stop." Although she loved his tongue and the way he was sucking her pussy, she wanted him inside of her badly.

Suddenly Lawrence came up from eating her pussy. He climbed up her body until his dick was right in her face. He looked down as he rubbed his erection all over her face. She grabbed it and took him inside her mouth. She gave him serious head for a while but didn't want to make him cum.

"Fuck me. Put this big dick inside me and fuck me, Lawrence."

He gave her what she asked for. Pushing her legs in the air, he slid inside her nice and deep. She was too far gone. She came as soon as he got all the way inside her tight pussy. It was all that she wanted it to be. The orgasm was so intense as he stroked her pussy with long, slow strokes. She began to shake and make sounds that only made him fuck her deeper. Her moans got louder with every stroke. The stroking was out of this world. He was pulling out, almost all the way, and then digging back inside her with force and grunts. He wanted to cum. She could tell. Every time he slammed inside of her it made her climax more intense.

She moaned, "Oh shit, I'm cummin' again! I'm cummin' again...you are fuckin' me so hard...so deep...don't stop, please don't stop!"

"Fuck me back you sexy bitch!" He was pounding her pussy now.

"Oh yeah, talk to me like that." She threw the pussy back at him. She was turned on by the way he called her a sexy bitch.

"You, like that, bitch? You like the way I'm fucking you?"

"Oh God, Yes! Yes! Yes! Yes!"

"I knew it, I knew you would love this big dick. I knew you would love the way I fuck you."

"Sssssss, yes, I love it, daddy. I love it! Fuck me harder." No Draws closed her eyes and squeezed her pussy tight, grinding her hips upward. "Uh, uh, uh..." The sex was getting her high. The dick had her close to passing out.

Lawrence pulled out of her pussy suddenly. She moaned in disappointment.

"What's wrong?"

Out of the blue he slipped inside of her wet ass with ease.

"Oh yeah, daddy." She accepted the dick in the ass and fucked back. She was so into it she would have let him put it anywhere. His dick had slipped right in from the wetness of her pussy.

"It's so good in my ass.... Ahhhh.... So good." Her moans were now deeper. "I'm about to cum again."

Lawrence was going hard now. He had his dream whore and he was sliding in and out of her ass making her moan like he was killing her.

"Take it bitch, take this dick you sexy bitch."

"Fuck me! Fuck me, oh God, fuck me harder! I want it harder!"

They went at it as if they were in battle until she felt him swell inside her ass. He growled as he fucked her faster and then pulled out of her ass and exploded on her stomach in a thick, warm stream of cum.

Out of breath, No Draws smiled and said, "You are so good, I see why your wife married you."

Snapping out of his sexual flashblack, Lawrence felt his erection at full strength.

No Draws saw the look on his face and could almost read his mind. With a smile and a sexy tone, she said, "What's on your mind, Lawrence?"

He laughed. "Just thinking about you showing me a good time."

No Draws winked. "That's my word."

The Aftermath

Just after 1:00pm, Lil Rose woke up in a Silver Spring, MD hotel room. A sexy brown-skinned girl was lying next to him. She was still dead to the world. Her name was Mimi, she ran with the Fuck'em Up Honeys. After all the drama at The Mad Chef, Lil Rose decided to hit the hotel and get some pussy. Mimi was the perfect candidate for some late night pill popping and go hard fucking. Lil Rose had spent more than a few nights in a hotel with Mimi.

Getting up to take a piss, Lil Rose grabbed his cell phone to see what calls he missed while he and Mimi were doing their thing. There were two messages from Marky and a few from different females. Taking a long stretch, Lil Rose rubbed his eyes and then went in the bathroom.

When he was done, he called Marky.

"What's up, moe?" Marky answered the phone. The sounds of the hood were in the background.

"Ain't shit. Still at the hotel wit' Mimi. Where you at?" Lil Rose asked.

"'Round the way. Aye, moe...you know Driver got smoked last night?"

"No bullshit?!" Lil Rose dropped his head in disappointment.

"On everything, kill, moe." Marky said. "Shorty got punished on Benning Road at a light. Everybody talkin' 'bout that shit."

The first person that came to Lil Rose's mind was Styles. He flashed back to how funny Styles was acting at The Mad Chef.

Marky continued, "All Driver's little men strapped up talkin' 'bout runnin' down on the nigga Styles."

"I was just thinkin' 'bout that nigga. I think he the one that put that work in. We'll talk about it when I get back 'round the way." Lil Rose didn't feel comfortable talking about beefs over the phone.

Marky said, "You know that was Styles' little youngin', Eric that the police punished last night."

"Oh yeah, damn, I ain't know that. I was tryin' to get the fuck outta there when I heard them shots goin' off."

"Aye, moe, you better check out the news. They been talkin' 'bout that Mad Chef shit all day. Some bitches got smoked too. Shit got real live out there, moe."

Lil Rose said, "Shit be like that sometimes." He paused for a second, thinking about Driver. He had a lot of love for the young nigga and was fucked up that he had to get smoked.

"Look though, let me get myself together. I'ma catch you when I get around the way."

"Catch you then, moe." Marky ended the call.

Lil Rose shut his phone and shook his head as he thought about Driver.

Inside Tonio's basement, the movie "Training Day" was playing on the fifty-inch flat screen. He, Vida and Tia were sitting around eating pizza. Tonio was impressed by the job Vida and Tia did on Romel and Manny. Now it was his turn to look out for them and get them out of the country.

On the table beside the pizza box sat two fresh passports for Vida and Tia and plane tickets to London, England. Tonio's contact had it all laid out for $50,000. Once the girls made it safely to the U.K, another contact was to set them up with all they needed upon arrival. After that they were on their own.

Vida sipped some Pepsi and said, "Aye, Tonio, you sure the whole London hook-up is safe?"

Tonio nodded.

"Trust me, ma. The peoples that I'm dealin' wit' charge $15,000 to get Mexicans in and out of the country everyday. You two are in good hands. I got you."

Vida was uncomfortable about the whole London move. What would she and Tia do if they even made it to London safely? What if Tonio's contact didn't come through on his end once they were in London? Countless questions raced through Vida's head.

Tonio could tell Vida was worried about the game plan.

"Vida, don't worry. I ain't no small time nigga. I'm a big boy. I got your back. Shit gon' work out just fine. You and Tia gon' disappear without a trace, ma."

Tia couldn't wait to jump on a plane out of the country.

"So run the game plan by me one more time, Tonio." Tia bit into a fresh slice of pizza. "Once we get to London, we look for a Nigerian by the name of Baron, right?"

"He will be looking for you two, soon as you get through customs." Tia said.

Vida sighed. She was nervous but she was ready to do what she had to do. It was all or nothing at this point. "I'm ready to make it happen." She said.

Tia looked at Tonio and said, "So you sure we gon' be straight on paper once we get over there?"

"I'ma make sure y'all well taken care of. Believe that, that's my word." Tonio assured.

Tia shrugged. "Cool, I'm ready to get the show on the road."

Tonio winked. "By tomorrow you and Vida gon' be on your way to the U.K. wit' new names and a clean past."

Vida smiled. Tonio sounded confident. She just hoped he was right.

The news was on the TV in Tera's apartment. The top story was the violence at The Mad Chef club. Eric's murder, at the hands of PG County police was the focus. The police justified killing Eric by directing all of the attention at the young female he murdered by the name of Shontae Washington. Summer's murder was being connected with

Eric as well. The public was calling for The Mad Chef to be shut down because of all the violence, since this wasn't the first incident there.

Shaking her head, Paris said, "Damn, that bitch-ass nigga killed Shonate." She felt like it was her fault that Shontae got murdered since she sent her inside the club to go at Most Wanted.

"That's fucked up." Tera said, sitting on the sofa next to Paris. She felt the pain of losing Shontae. She and Paris had been friends with Shontae since the 6th grade.

"It was a lot of killin' last night…Mufuckas is playin' for keeps." Paris said.

"I see…I know Lil Rose and them gon' go off about Driver."

"Hell yeah. I think they gon' end up goin' at the nigga Styles."

"Why you say that?" Tera asked.

"You know Driver fucked Styles' car up and then pulled a 'K' on 'em."

"I ain't know that."

Paris shrugged. "You gotta keep your ear to the streets."

She grabbed the remote and flicked the TV to BET's videos. T.I. was doing his thing.

"Aye, is it me or was Lala actin' funny after I smoked that bitch Summer?" Paris asked.

"She was actin' funny, she ain't feeling that gun play shit." Tera said.

Paris was rubbed the wrong way by Lala because Lala was acting scared after Summer's murder. Lala told Tera to drop her off at home as soon as they got back to D.C.

"I don't trust her, Tera." Paris said. "She was actin' too damn scared."

"Don't trip off that shit, girl. Lala will get over that shit. Just give her some space."

Paris thought about the situation for a hot second. "I don't think Lala can hold water if the police question us about that shit."

Tera gave Paris a funny look. "So what you sayin', Paris?"

Paris shrugged. "I don't trust her…you saw how she was actin'."

Tera waved Paris off.

"You trippin', boo. On everything." She walked to the kitchen.

Paris sucked her teeth. "I ain't trippin'." She rolled her eyes.

Inside Styles' posh bedroom under the Ralph Lauren sheets naked, he and Samara were worn out from hours of sexing. Styles had so much on his mind, things that were stressing him out, so he fucked Samara like he was mad at her as if he was trying to kill the pussy. She enjoyed every minute of it.

Styles was not new to the murder game. He'd pulled the trigger a number of times. Taking a life was no big deal to him. However, he kept having flashbacks of killing Driver. He couldn't get the sight out of his head. No matter how hard he fucked Samara, no matter how much and how loud she moaned, Styles couldn't get rid of the mental image of what the Desert Eagle did to Driver.

Aside from that, Styles was fucked up about how the police had done his youngin' Eric. Death was the only thing that was certain in the streets.

Sleeping as a woman did after mind-blowing sex, Samara's head was resting on Styles' chest. He turned his head toward her and took a deep breath. He loved the way her Victoria's Secret body wash made her smell.

His cell phone vibrated on the nightstand. He grabbed it, not waking Samara and answered it. "What's up, Eyes?"

Eyes was real close with Eric.

"What's good, moe?" Eyes said, Lil Wayne's rapping on a track could be heard in the background.

"Shit, layin' in for the day. I'm jive fucked up about that shit wit' Eric last night."

"Yeah, me too. Shit been all on the news." Someone in the car interrupted Eyes and he exchanged a few words.

"Yeah, my bad. Aye, moe, you know niggas done came through here shootin' twice today."

"Oh yeah?" Styles kept his voice low.

"Yeah, Creek said it was them youngins from Saratoga…Niggas think The Park (Congress Park) had somethin' to do wit' the young nigga Driver gettin' punished last night."

Styles sighed. "If it ain't one thing it's another. Where you at, slim?"

"Me and Creek on our way uptown to holla at my man real quick. We gon' be back around the way in a minute." Eyes said.

"I'll meet you around the Park a little later on."

"Bet." Eyes ended the call.

Styles shut his cell phone. He thought of how one murder led to the next one. It seemed like the shit never stopped. At least not in D.C., drama was never ending, and one wrong move would get a nigga put in the dirt.

Samara's hand stroking Styles' manhood grabbed his attention. He looked down and saw a smile on her face. She was awake and the first thing she did was reach for his dick. Up and down, her soft hand stroked him to a strong erection, one that she wanted inside of her again. Her nipples hardened. She sent chills up Styles' spine with her electric touch. He rubbed her breasts and squeezed her hard nipples, making her hiss with pleasure. She shivered with passion and ecstasy, as Styles' erection grew harder and larger right between her fingers. Unimaginable wetness grew between Samara's sexy legs.

Styles leaned down and kissed Samara, sliding his tongue inside her mouth. He tried to focus on the pleasure Samara was pushing his way, but Styles kept thinking about Driver and Eric. Death was on his mind hard.

Samara moaned, "I want you so bad." She kissed him again. The kiss was intense, as she continued to stroke his dick. Styles licked her chin, neck and down to her hard nipples. Her moans got louder and she was in need of what he was doing to her. She let his dick go and he made his way between her legs, never taking his tongue off her skin.

He parted her legs and began to taste her, sucking and nibbling on her like a honeydew melon. She began slowly pushing her pussy up into his face, wanting more pleasure, more tongue, more licking, and more sucking. He slid his hands under her soft ass, squeezed it and pulled her pussy closer to his face. Her moans grew deeper and louder.

Samara moaned. She stretched her arms out wide and grabbed the bed sheets to try to stop herself from going crazy. Her eyes rolled back in her head.

She moaned, "Yeah...Yes...Oh yeah, don't stop, baby." She shook her head side to side. "Lick all over it, baby. Eat this pussy...Ohhh yesss." Her body began to shake. Styles' slurping, sucking and biting was pushing her over the edge.

"Styles! Oh my God! I'm cumin!"

As he continued to eat her pussy, thoughts of murder continued to flood his mind.

Takin' Flight

Police were looking for Vida and Tia everywhere. The FBI was all over the case now as well. Their pictures were still all over the news and CNN. Everybody in the D.C. area was talking about how Vida and Tia were sure to do life in prison or even face the death penalty since police officers had been murdered in connection with their murder spree.

Anxiety covered Vida's face, although she was trying her best to look normal. Her palms were sweaty. Her heart was racing. She kept tapping her foot. The nervousness she felt just would not go away. Maybe she would feel better if Tia was sitting next to her on the British Airways flight to London. However, Tia was seated a few seats down the aisle. They had made it onto the plane. Their IDs and passports worked fine. They acted as if they weren't together, at least as they boarded the plane. Now they were in the air, leaving the U.S. behind. Vida couldn't believe it. She was surprised and relieved that getting out of the country was as easy as Tonio said it would be. Yet and still, Vida was fearful of what she and Tia would be in store for once the plane landed. For now she was still free, on the run but still free, and that's all that mattered.

Sitting two seats to the left in the aisle seat was a smooth, brown-skinned man in a Gucci suit. He wore Gucci glasses and was clean cut like a lawyer. Vida hadn't said a word to the dude, although she did give him a fake smile and a nod when he took his seat.

Trying her best to stay to herself during the flight, Vida focused her attention on the urban novel she'd grabbed to keep her company during the eight hours she would be in the air. Jason Poole's novel, *Larceny*, grabbed her attention when she read the back of it and saw that it was about two friends that go through a world of struggles together. It made Vida think of herself and Tia.

Moments later, Tia walked up, holding the seats to keep her balance, and whispered, "Excuse me, are you still interested in the back?"

Vida caught on quickly. "Yeah thanks."

Vida excused herself and slid by the dude in the Gucci suit. She followed Tia back to her window seat. Tia had three seats all to herself.

Tia slid over to the window and winked at Vida.

"Come on, sit down. I ain't sitting back here by myself for the whole flight."

Vida smiled slightly and shook her head as she took a seat close to the aisle.

Looking out the window, Tia whispered, "We on our way, Vee."

Vida nodded with a sigh. "Tonio looked out like he said he was. Now we gotta figure out what we gon' do in London."

"It don't even matter, Vee. We ain't sittin' in no jail cell."

Vida agreed. "You right about that."

"Besides, if we can survive in them D.C. streets, we can make it anywhere, boo. You know that."

Vida didn't say anything. She thought about Moe-Moe and Bloody for a second. Sadness squeezed her heart and she fought to shake it off.

Tia's IPod was playing Lil Wayne through the headset around her neck. As she nodded her head to the beat, she said, "What you thinkin' 'bout, Vee?"

Vida shook her head.

"Everything. Never in a million years would I think we would be on a damn plane to London, on the run for murder. I had so many other plans for my future… I really wanted to do right. I wanted to make my grandmother proud." Vida looked like she wanted to cry.

Tia rubbed Vida's arm with care and understanding. "Don't do that, Vee. Don't beat yourself up about this shit. We ain't ask for this, it came our way. You hear me, Vee?"

Vida nodded, taking a deep breath.

"We gon' deal wit' this shit, whatever comes wit' it we gon' deal wit'. Me and you, boo. Til' death do us part. It is what it is, Vee."

"You right, Tee." Vida said.

Tia gave Vida a warm smile. "We gon' be fine. We gon' disappear and make a new life far away from all that bullshit back home."

A hot second later, drink service came down the aisle. Vida ordered a bottle of white wine, something to mellow her out while Tia ordered Coke. They sat and spoke about what they would do in London for a while, neither one of them had a real idea of what was to come.

After sipping her wine for a second, Vida felt a little more at ease. She tried to find comfort in the fact that they had made it out of the U.S., at least.

Tia looked at Vida and said, "When we get over there, all we gotta do is hit the hood. People from the hood understand people from the hood, that's all over the world, Vee."

Vida laughed.

"Girl, you a trip."

With Lil Wayne still pumping through her headset, Tia said, "No bullshit, Vee. Real recognize real. You know that. No matter where we go, we gon' always be hood bitches, bitches from the streets. We could be in D.C. or anywhere else in the world, it don't matter. We gon' be 'aight, Vee."

Vida nodded. "I feel you."

"You remember Kobi, from First and Kennedy?"

"Yeah, I remember him. I remember both twins, Kobi and Kareem…I used to like Corkey from up there." Vida said.

"Remember when Kobi went on the run for that Kennedy street shit?" Tia raised her eyebrows getting to her point.

"Yeah I remember that. I just read about it again in the Don Diva magazine."

"Look how Kobi rolled out on they ass…He dipped on 'em, hit Russia, Egypt, Kenya, Tanzania, he ain't play no games. Kobi was hitting hoods in Africa. They say they was over there robbin' shit and everything. The world is a ghetto, Vee. Wherever we go, we gon' be 'aight."

Vida thought about what Tia was saying for a second.

"You got a point there. But on the real, how long you think we can run? It ain't like we sittin' on millions of dollars."

"Fuck that shit, we gon' run as long as we have to, Vee, and we gon' do whatever it takes to make it work. Bullshit ain't nothin'." Tia said.

Hours later, anxiety ran through Vida's body like the effects of an intravenous drug. She was nervous again. The plane had landed in London. It was show time. She had to calm herself and get ready to deal with customs.

Tia was just waking up, she was stretching and yawning. Music was still pumping though her headset at low volume.

The smooth, brown-skinned dude that wore the Gucci suit passed Vida on his way back from the bathroom. Her heart skipped a beat when she laid eyes on him. He had a folded newspaper under his arm, *The Washington Post*. Vida was sure she and Tia were in the paper, pictures and all. Although they both looked very different, Vida was still extremely nervous.

Vida looked at Tia and whispered, "Aye, Tee, why the bamma in the Gucci suit just walked by wit' *The Washington Post*."

Tia looked around but the dude was gone down the aisle.

"Don't worry 'bout it, Vee. We here now, that nigga don't got no idea who we are."

Vida shrugged. "Yeah, 'aight…I just thought we was gettin' far away from that shit and then I see this nigga wit' the Post. I wonder who the fuck he is."

"He ain't payin' us no attention. Let's just stay focused and worry about gettin' off this plane." Tia said.

Moments later everyone was told that they could get up.

Vida's mind was still on that Washington Post. A newspaper that had made a long trip from the U.S. to the U.K. A newspaper that surely had her name and picture in it. The past finds ways to follow a person. Yesterdays were always one step behind the present.

Tia could see the nervousness on Vida's face.

"Chill, Vee. We cool. We got this. Try to look normal." She said.

Vida smiled. She got with the program. "I really liked this book." She patted the *Larceny* book on her lap. She'd read the whole thing. "Jason Poole can write."

"Oh yeah?" Tia pretended to be interested. "Ain't slim from D.C.?"

"Yeah, but he locked up right now, in the feds."

Vida kept her eyes open for any sign of something that didn't look right on the plane. Not that she or Tia could do anything about it, they had no weapons. If law enforcement were to get on their ass it would be all she wrote.

Along with the crowd of passengers heading for the front of the plane, Vida and Tia headed into the unknown. They were both nervous but kept their game faces on. Carrying backpacks, they made it off the plane. It felt like all eyes were on them. Although they were all the way across the Atlantic Ocean, every white man in a suit looked like the FBI to Vida and Tia.

Scores of people headed for customs. It was like walking city blocks in downtown D.C. People upon people, jet lagged, all heading in the same direction on moving sidewalks and all.

Finally, they hit customs Vida's and Tia's heart beat faster as they looked around, standing in a long line for non-U.K. citizens. Slowly, people were dealt with one by one, going on about their business in the U.K.

Vida whispered to Tia, "I'm nervous as shit." She flashed an easy smile.

With a light laugh, as if Vida told a joke, Tia said, "Me too, Vee but we good. All we gotta do is stay focused."

Tia's stomach bubbled and her hands trembled slightly as she watched custom agents check passports and question people that wanted to enter the European country.

"It's feds all over the place." Tia said.

"I'm hip." Vida said as she checked out her fake passport, praying that it got her through customs. In London, her name would be Dawn Jones—Tia's would be Carmen Ward.

"I'm sweatin'." Tia whispered.

Vida smiled. Her nerves had her jumpy. Moments later Vida was face to face with a blue-eyed customs agent. She was tense and nervous but she kept her cool.

Tia looked on, hoping that all went well.

Vida handed the agent her passport. He looked at the passport, then back to Vida and back at the passport. He asked her a few questions. Vida played it cool, answered the questions like it was nothing and then she was free to go. Just like that.

Tia was like: Yes!

Vida walked a nice distance away and then stopped and waited on Tia, praying everything went as planned.

Tia was directed to another customs agent, a woman. Vida watched closely. Tia handed the agent her passport. She and the agent exchanged a few words. The agent seemed to be new; she had another agent coaching her. After more questions, Tia was asked to step to the side and follow the female agent. A tall male agent followed behind them. Tia looked back at Vida with a nervous look on her face.

"Oh my God." Vida whispered to herself. Her heart dropped. What could she do? She felt helpless. She wanted to run after Tia.

For some reason it seemed like more police appeared out of thin air.

Vida was frozen. She couldn't move, even though something inside her was screaming: Run! Run! Run! Get the fuck out of Gatwick Airport!

"Excuse me, miss." A male voice said from behind Vida.

Tradin' Shots

Saratoga Avenue was dead. Nothing was going down. The police had just left the scene, they had responded to calls of gunfire. Young niggas from Congress Park had just come through bussin' that hot shit in retaliation for Driver's men coming through Congress Park shooting earlier. Driver's little crew went through Congress Park spraying bullets twice within a three-hour span; they hit a nigga in the back but didn't kill him. The Congress Park young niggas didn't kill anyone either, although they punished the front of an apartment building and fucked up a few parked cars. Tension was high now.

Coming out of the dark cut beside the building, Mechanic headed down Saratoga Avenue. He looked at the destruction the Congress Park youngins left behind and was glad he didn't get caught in the gunfire.

The sound of a car coming down the street caught Mechanic's attention. It was a blue Toyota Camry. The car pulled up and parked in front of the building that had been shot up. Lil Rose stepped out the car in a deep-blue LRG shirt. He looked around at the aftermath of the gunfire.

Mechanic looked at his nephew noticing his glares.

"Yeah, baby boy, niggas came through here like it was downtown Baghdad. Shit sounded like machine guns." He said.

"How long ago?" Lil Rose stepped onto the sidewalk.

"Bout an hour or so. The police left a few minutes ago." Mechanic took a long pull on his Newport that was down to the butt. "I'm surprised ain't nobody get hit wit' all that damn shooting."

"Damn." Lil Rose shook his head. He already had an idea that the shooting was connected with Driver's little crew blasting up Congress Park.

"Shit off the chain...I heard little Driver got killed. This shit got somethin' to do wit' that?" Mechanic plucked his cigarette butt in the street.

Lil Rose shrugged. "I ain't sure, moe."

"You seen Paris?" Mechanic asked.

"Nah, why?" Lil Rose pulled out his cell phone to call Marky.

"Detectives came by my spot askin' questions 'bout my car bein' used in some shootin'. I let Paris use my car...I hope she ain't got me caught up in no bullshit, man." Mechanic looked up and down the dark street.

Lil Rose raised his eyebrows. By this time he already knew Paris murdered Summer.

"What did the detectives say?"

"They was talkin' 'bout somebody jumped out my car and killed some girl outside a club in PG. I'm tryin' to holla at Paris and find out what the hell's goin' on."

Lil Rose shook his head, he knew Paris was trippin' to smoke a bitch in front of countless witnesses. For a second Lil Rose felt bad for giving her the Beretta with the silencer on it.

Giving his uncle a serious look, Lil Rose said, "What you say to the detectives?"

"You know me nephew. Don't know shit when the feds askin' questions." Mechanic said, never looking Lil Rose in the eyes.

"I'ma holla at Paris soon as I see her, I'ma ask her what's good." Lil Rose adjusted the pistol on his waistband.

Rubbing his chin, looking uncomfortable, Mechanic said, "On another tip, that Panamanian nigga, Lito, was 'round here earlier askin' questions about that robbery again."

"Oh yeah," Lil Rose was becoming concerned more and more about Lito. He was thinking that he was going to have to go ahead and smoke that dude.

"No bullshit, nephew. The nigga asked about you."

"Asked what?!" Lil Rose snapped.

"Wanted to know who you was."

"Who was the nigga talkin' to?"

"A few smokers…I just wanted to put you on point." Mechanic said.

"Good lookin', let me know if the nigga come through here again."

"You got that nephew." Mechanic headed down the street.

Lil Rose headed inside the apartment building, calling Marky on his cell.

Paris sat on the sofa in her living room in a white T-shirt and a pair of gray Prada shorts. She had a lot on her mind. It bothered her that Shontae got killed behind the drama with Most Wanted. Shontae was a real bitch, as far as Paris was concerned. "Damn." Paris shook her head and looked back at the TV, watching, "The Wire". Summer crossed her mind. I showed that bitch, she thought. Not one bit of remorse lived in Paris' heart for what she did to Summer. For all she cared, all them Most Wanted bitches could eat a bullet, one after the other.

A knock at the door surprised Paris and made her jump. She made her way to the door and looked through the peephole. It was Lil Rose.

She opened the door. "What's up, boy?"

Lil Rose stepped inside. "What's on your mind, Paris?"

She shut the door and smiled.

"What you talkin' 'bout, Rose?"

He gave her a look like: cut the jokes out!

She laughed and walked by him throwing her ass enticingly and took her seat on the sofa. "What you talkin' 'bout?" She continued to play dumb.

"I thought you was smarter than that, Paris." Lil Rose took a seat on the sofa beside her. "Why the fuck would you smoke a bitch in front of all them witnesses? You think ain't nobody gon' tell on your ass?"

"Ain't nobody see me...It was too much drama out that bitch."

Lil Rose shook his head in amazement and laughed a little bit.

"You can't be that naïve." He gave her a serious look, it showed concern but it was dead serious. "You know detectives been to Mechanic's house askin' questions?"

That scared Paris and it showed on her face.

"Yeah!" Lil Rose nodded and raised his eyebrows for emphasis. "Them peoples askin' questions. This ain't like you fuckin' a bitch up or slicin' a bitch wit' a razor. We talkin' 'bout murder and you smoked the bitch out PG County—them peoples ain't playin' 'bout no shit like that. Kill, that's on everything."

Paris looked nervous, she said, "What did Mechanic tell 'em?"

"He said he ain't tell 'em nothin' but my point is that they askin' questions 'bout the shit and they ain't even supposed to be able to do that, they ain't supposed to know shit."

Paris gave Lil Rose's words some deep thought and said, "So what should I do now?"

Lil Rose's phone vibrated in his pocket. He pulled it out and saw it was Marky. He looked at Paris and shrugged. "I don't know what to tell you, Paris." He then answered the phone.

"Marky, what's up, moe?"

"It's all good. I already heard 'bout that shit that went down around the way…you know we gon' have to step up and straighten that out." Marky said, he sounded like he was smoking.

"No doubt, I'ma holla at you about that soon as soon as I get to your spot, so stay put. Cool?"

"Ain't no problem wit' that. See you when you get here." Marky ended the call.

Lil Rose did the same and put his phone in his pocket. He glanced at Paris. She now had a nervous and paranoid look on her cute face.

"You thinkin' 'bout what I said, huh?"

She nodded. "Yeah. I gotta do somethin', Rose."

"Who saw you do the shit?"

"Lala and Tera was in the car wit' me but the bitches that was wit' Summer started runnin' soon as I started shootin', but they really ain't see me like that. It was too dark out there."

Lil Rose shook his head and scoffed at her words. It was no doubt in his mind that some of the girls with Summer had gotten a good look at Paris.

"Look here, I ain't gon' pull no punches wit' you. Can you really trust Lala and Tera when it comes to facin' murder charges?"

Paris said nothing for a second.

"That's what I thought." Lil Rose threw his hands in the air.

"Tera can hold water…I'm sure of it, but Lala was actin' jive funny. I don't know 'bout her."

Lil Rose sighed. "Don't get me wrong, baby girl, I gots love for Lala and Tera, but three can only keep a secret if two are dead. That's how it goes, Paris. The old timers taught me that when I was a little nigga."

She nodded in understanding. "I ain't worried 'bout Tera, she would never tell on me, we been arrested together for cuttin' bitches a rack of times. She can stand tall. But as far as Lala…I don't know…"

"Could you kill her if you had to? Could you look her in the eyes and kill her?" Lil Rose gave her a serious look, staring deep into her eyes.

"Yeah," Paris nodded. "I think I could do it. I gotta lot of love for Lala...That's my girl but if she's a weak link I'm sure I could get rid of her ass."

Lil Rose stood up to leave.

"You might have to do that." He shrugged. "What you do wit' that hamma?"

"I still got it."

Lil Rose shook his head. "Let me get that pistol, I'ma get rid of it."

Paris went to her room and returned with the Beretta with the silencer on it. She handed it to Lil Rose.

Unscrewing the silencer, Lil Rose slipped it in his pocket and then tucked the pistol in the small of his back.

"I gotta go, you need to chill. I'll be back through here before the night is over."

Paris gave Lil Rose a hug and a kiss. He squeezed her ass. She smiled and said, "I want some of that dick when you come back, too."

"You got that." He winked.

Lil Rose pulled up in the parking lot of the 7-Eleven on Annapolis Road in New Carrollton, MD. He parked beside a late model Nissan Sentra. His driver's side door faced the driver's side door of the Sentra. Behind the wheel of the Sentra was a young brown-skinned dude by the name of Rome.

Rome was from Landover, MD, he and Lil Rose were cool and had met a few years back when they were locked up at Boys Village, a juvenile detention center for adolescent boys.

The windows of both cars came down at the same time. Rome said, "What's up, moe?"

"On the grind, you know how it go." Lil Rose looked around the parking lot for any signs of the police. Nothing seemed out of place. Smoothly, he got out of his car with a Safeway shopping bag in his hand. He slid up on the window of Rome's car and dropped 1001 grams of powder cocaine in his lap.

Rome felt the weight of the coke hit his lap. He trusted Lil Rose, and he knew it was a brick in the Safeway bag. He handed Lil Rose a brown paper bag containing $20,000.

"Good lookin' out, Rose. If you run across another move like this one make sure you holla at me. I'm payin' twenty-five a brick right now. You saved a nigga five Gs."

"I'll holla back at you if I come up like this here again but this might be a one time thing, moe."

Rome gave Lil Rose a pound. "I'm gone." He pulled off.

Lil Rose jumped back in his car and looked inside the paper bag Rome had given him. It looked like $20,000 but he would count it all at Marky's apartment. Stuffing the paper bag under his seat, Lil Rose ran inside the 7-Eleven to grab some Backwoods.

Coming out of the store, Lil Rose locked eyes with Styles who was stepping out of his beat-up Lexus. They both stopped in their tracks. Driver's murder came to Lil Rose's mind. He was sure Styles was behind the move.

In some strange way, it was like Styles could read Lil Rose's mind. In the blink of an eye, Styles went for his pistol.

Lil Rose dropped the backwoods and went for his Smith & Wesson .40.

A young female walking by screamed and pulled her young son to the ground, covering him with her body.

Gunfire exploded!

Boom! Boom! Boom!

Blow! Blow! Blow!

Then the sounds of gunfire mixed together became deadly thunder that shook the 7-Eleven parking lot.

Bullets flew in all directions. Bullets crashed through the glass of the front of the store window.

Hot lead ripped into Lil Rose's chest and left shoulder, knocking him against the window of the 7-Eleven. Four more slugs slammed into his chest.

Styles got his shots off first and never let Lil Rose get his shit together.

Lil Rose fell to the ground. Styles finished him. With two to the head.

Styles jumped in his car and went flying out the parking lot.

Inside Cee-Cee's brother's apartment, she and Bria were sneaking through his closet looking for his Mac-10 sub machine gun. They planned to go after Paris and the Hell Razor Honeys for Summer's murder. The game was on another level now, gunplay was involved. Since Cee-Cee's brother wouldn't let her use his Mac-10 to go after Paris, she and Bria decided to swipe the joint and put it back when they were done since he was in New York on a drug run.

"I got it." Cee-Cee said, holding the heavy gun with both hands. "It's loaded too."

Glancing at the sub-machine gun, Bria said, "You know how to use that joint?"

"Hell yeah," Cee-Cee nodded. "My brother showed me how to use this bitch. I know what I'm doin'." She stuffed the gun inside her large Prada handbag. "We gon' spray them bitches for what they did to Summer." Cee-Cee's voice cracked with sadness but she refused to cry anymore over Summer's death.

Cee-Cee and Summer were like sisters and had been so since they were kids. When Summer's mother was on drugs, Cee-Cee's mother took Summer in and treated her like a daughter for years. Summer called Cee-Cee's mother her mother. So losing Summer was not just losing one of her Most Wanted girls, it was really losing a sister as far as Cee-Cee was concerned, and Paris wasn't going to get away with that shit.

Fixing up the closet, Bria said, "So it's just me and you?"

Cee-Cee nodded. "Yeah, we ain't gon' let nobody know what we doin'. It's between you, Bria and me. You got that?"

"Got you, Cee. I got you, I'm wit' you all the way. Let's get these Hell Razor bitches."

Samara was relaxing in Styles' bed watching, "The Wire". Her mind was on Vida and Tia. She wondered how they were doing and where they were. She prayed the feds didn't catch them but how long could they run? Samara had read in the *Washington Post* that Vida and Tia could face death if they were arrested, their whole situation was unreal to Samara. It was like a movie. Even though she was pissed off when Vida sent Bloody to Styles' apartment with a gun, Samara would never wish for harm to come to Vida or Tia. They were her girls for life.

Hearing the front door of the apartment open, Samara knew Styles was home. Wearing nothing but a long white T-shirt she went to meet him. As soon as she got to the living room she smelled a strong, funny smell. She didn't know it but it was the gunpowder that was on Styles' clothes.

Styles stood in the middle of the living room with an intense look on his face. The look on his face spooked Samara, however, the scar across his cheekbone alarmed her.

Rushing over to him with concern, Samara said, "Styles, what happened to you, baby?!"

A bullet grazed Styles' face in the shoot out with Lil Rose.

Pushing Samara's hands away from his face, Styles snapped.

"I'm okay!" He sounded cold and mean. Samara wasn't used to that.

"Call my car in stolen."

"What's wrong wit' you?! Tell me somethin'!" Samara shouted.

"Sam!!" Styles barked, making her jump. "Just call the fuckin' car in stolen! Okay?!"

Samara rushed to the phone.

Styles went to the bathroom to work on his graze wound. While in the bathroom he thought about how close he came to death. Bullets had flown by his head on two different occasions in less than twenty-four hours. Death was coming too close for comfort. Lil Rose almost murdered my ass, Styles thought. Maybe it's time for me to lay low for a second, he told himself.

Coming out of the bathroom, Styles ran right into Samara's intense gaze. She now had an attitude.

With her hands on her hips, she said, "Are you gonna tell me what the fuck happened to you?"

Styles shook his head and sighed. Samara wasn't helping and for real she was just stressing him out.

"You don't need to know!" Styles shouted he was beyond frustrated.

"What the fuck you mean I don't need to know?!" She shouted back

Pissed off, Styles shouted, "Your homie, Lil Rose, tried to kill me!!"

Samara's mouth dropped open in surprise. She was shocked. She had love for Lil Rose.

"Satisfied now?" Styles shook his head. "The young nigga tried to kill me and I smoked his ass."

Samara shook her head.

"Oh my God… I can't believe this shit. Why did Rose try to kill you?"

Styles told her, pulling no punches.

Taking a deep breath, Samara said, "So what's next?"

Styles shrugged. "Ain't no tellin'."

London

Victoria Station, thousands of miles away from Washington D.C., meant thousands of miles away from money, murder, and drugs. All of that was on the other side of the Atlantic Ocean. Victoria Station was dominated by British culture. Masses of people were moving at a swift pace as if they were in a rush to get somewhere. Some were rushing up to the streets, others were rushing down to the trains.

Vida, Tia and a Nigerian by the name of Baron were on the escalator on their way up to the streets and up into the heat of London during the summer.

Baron was tall, dark as night, and handsome. His accent was a smooth British one. He was the contact that was to meet Vida and Tia and make sure they were taken care of once they made it to London. Baron didn't know Tonio personally; his only contact with Tonio was through one of his business associates in New York. Baron was a man of many connections.

Tia was still shaken up from the customs scare. She was picked for a random search by a rookie customs agent but was free to go after a pat down and inspection of her backpack.

Vida didn't know what to do when Tia was led away by customs agents, she thought the worst for a second. That is until Baron stepped on the Scene and gave her hope that Tia would be okay and in the end she was.

Now Vida and Tia were on their way to a Tower Hill safe house with Baron. Anxiety still consumed Vida and Tia but they had made it to London. That was a huge plus. All they had to do at this point was lay low and do all they could to avoid attention.

They jumped in a cab and put Victoria Station behind them. Vida and Tia sat beside one another. Baron sat facing them in the British cab. He was dressed in Gucci jeans and a white tank top. The gym was a spot he played on the regular. Diamonds danced around his Rolex. Prada shades kept the sun out of his eyes. He eyed Vida and Tia, they were both beautiful but it was something about Vida that had imprisoned his attention.

Baron smiled a bright white smile and said, "You two beautiful ladies can take it easy now. You are far away from whatever troubles that brought you to the U.K." His British accent wasn't hard to understand at all. He could see that Vida and Tia were still nervous. He didn't know exactly what they were running from back in the U.S. but whatever it was, as far as he was concerned, was all behind them.

Vida and Tia looked at each other and then at Baron and smiled. If he only knew what kind of shit they were in back home, he would understand why they werc still ncrvous.

"It's gon' take us a minute to get used to bein' here, main man." Tia said and smiled.

Baron nodded with a handsome smile.

"I completely understand, so which one of you is Dawn?"

"Me." Vida said, on her toes.

Baron looked at Tia and said, "I take it that you must be Carmen?"

Tia winked. "That's me." She was looking out the window at all that was London. Never in a million years did she think she'd be in London on the run for murder.

"If you don't mind me asking, do you ladies have plans...after you leave the safe house, I mean?" Baron asked. He was only paid to give Vida and Tia somewhere to stay for a month.

"Not really, we'll figure that out real soon." Tia said.

Baron nodded. "I understand."

Vida's attention was out the window looking at all the different people in the streets of London. It seemed like all races were jammed in one place. Germans, Russians, Africans, many speaking French, as far as Vida had seen. There were young Europeans wearing T-shirts with 50 Cent and Jay-Z on the front.

Baron saw that Vida's mind was thousands of miles away. To him, it was something very intriguing about her. Looking at Tia, he said, "Your friend doesn't talk much, I see."

"She's been through a lot in the past few days." Tia rubbed Vida's back, knowing she was thinking about Moe-Moe and Bloody. Moe-Moe and Bloody weighed heavy on Tia's heart as well but she was able to deal with death better than Vida.

Baron's cell phone came to life with a 50 Cent ring tone. He pulled the phone from his pocket and checked the number.

"Excuse me for one second, Carmen." He answered the call.

Tia and Vida paid close attention to Baron's conversation. He was very careful with his words, he had the shrewdness of a man that knew how to evade conspiracy investigations.

After the exchange of a few quick words he ended the call and slid the phone back inside his pocket. Looking at the backpacks Vida and Tia were traveling with, Baron said, "I see you two packed light."

Tia said, "Yeah, we was moving fast. We can get all we need here. You got money for us, right?"

"For sure," Baron nodded. "There's a nice bit of loot at the safe house for you two. Your peoples back in the states made sure everything was taken care of.

The Tower Hill Safe house was on a tiny little street in postal code EC3. It was in an apartment building that sat right across the street from a hotel that people were going in and out of.

Baron let Vida and Tia into the plush flat and then closed the door and hit the lights. The girls looked around and saw black leather furniture, a huge flat screen TV, and a serious sound system with speakers in every corner of the room. There were granite counters and marble floors. There were two bedrooms; one was converted into a workout space with a treadmill, weight machine and a punching bag that hung from the ceiling.

"This is where you will stay until you find somewhere permanent to stay." Baron said. "Have a seat, I'll be right back." He disappeared into the bedroom.

Vida sat on the sofa with her arms folded, looking uncomfortable. She studied the apartment.

"Vee, we good now, boo. We made it." She rubbed Vida's back.

Vida nodded, but didn't say a word for a second. Slowly, she looked at Tia and said, "We still gotta be careful over here…we don't know nobody and we can't trust a soul."

Tia nodded. "I feel you on that." She got up and walked to the window. From the window she could see the hotel across the street. Two police officers were walking down the peaceful street. "The police over here don't even carry pistols, Vee."

"I noticed on the way here." Vida said.

"That's some wild shit there. I wish I would let a fuckin' cop wit' no gun lock me up. Picture that."

Baron came back into the living room with a black suitcase. He laid it on its side on the floor and opened it. Inside, Vida and Tia could see stacks and stacks of British currency.

"How much money is that?" Tia asked.

"Fifty-thousand pounds." He said.

Vida and Tia gave each other questioning looks. Baron smiled.

"It's close to a hundred-thousand dollars in U.S. currency…a pound is about two U.S. dollars."

Vida smiled and made a frustrated sound.

"I guess we got it made…we're set for life." She said sarcastically.

"I know how you feel but this will hold you for a little while. Baron said.

Tia shrugged. "It is what it is. We'll make it work."

"I'm not sure what you ladies were into back in the states but I can find you work here in London."

Vida raised her eyebrows.

"Work? What kind of work you talkin' 'bout?"

Looking back and forth between Vida and Tia, Baron said, "Just about anything, you name it, from legal to illegal. Whatever works. May I ask what you two were into back in the states?"

Tia glanced at Vida for a second to see how she felt about Baron's question.

"Honestly, we were into a little of everything, from legal to illegal but right now we're not tryin' to draw any attention to us." Vida said.

Baron nodded, he caught her vibe. "I understand. I'll check into a few things and let you know what comes up."

"Can you help us find another place to stay? I know we can only stay here for a few weeks." Tia said.

"That's not a problem. I have a female friend that'll show you around." Baron looked at his iced-out Rolex. "She's from the states also, she's been here for a few years now. She's a good friend to have, I'm sure you two will like her."

"Does your friend know about our situation?" Vida asked.

"She doesn't know the details, but she does know that you two are from the states and that you both are looking for a new beginning here."

Vida nodded. "I understand."

"Trust me, I'll make sure everything is smooth." Baron said. He pulled two travel cards from his pocket and sat them on the coffee table in front of Vida. "Those travel cards are good for a week. You can ride the tube with those, the tube gets you anywhere you want to go."

"You talkin' 'bout the train?" Tia said.

"It's called the tube." Baron said.

"You're goin' to get us new passports, right?" Vida asked.

He nodded. "I'll have those for you later on today."

"What about pistols? We need pistols. I don't feel safe without some steel. Bullshit ain't nothin'." Tia said.

Baron smiled. "Are you serious?"

"As a muthafucka." Tia said.

Baron laughed. "I can get you pistols. What kind do you want?"

"I like forty-fives, but I think a small nine will work. Get us two nines, they'll hold us." Tia said.

Baron nodded. "I'll make that happen."

He began to wonder about Vida and Tia and wanted to know what their story was.

The front door opened. Vida and Tia turned their attention to the woman that entered the apartment. She had smooth brown skin and couldn't be a day over twenty-five. She wore tight blue jeans and a white Prada T-shirt. Her silky hair was pulled into a ponytail.

Removing her big frame Prada shades, the young woman said, "Hello, did I interrupt you all?" Her accent was from the U.S., somewhere in the Dirty South.

"Monique, I was just talking about you, you're right on time. This is Dawn and Carmen." Baron said and waved toward Vida and Tia.

Monique smiled. "What's good, ladies?"

Tia nodded. "Ain't too much."

"Everything's cool." Vida said.

Baron's cell phone vibrated in his pocket. He pulled it out and answered the call as he headed toward the bathroom to speak in private.

Monique went to the refrigerator and grabbed a can of fresh orange juice.

"You two want something to drink?" She asked.

"Yeah, let me get one of them orange juices." Tia said.

Monique tossed a can to Tia.

"How about you, Dawn?" Monique asked.

Vida said, "I'm cool, I want some food for real. I'm hungry."

"I can take y'all to get some food." Monique took a seat in the deep leather chair to the right of Vida. "What are you in the mood for? They got everything over here. Burger King, Pizza Hut, just about everything they got back home."

Sitting beside Vida, sipping her orange juice, Tia said, "Yeah, I'd love some Pizza Hut."

Baron came back into the living room and said, "I've got to run. I'll be back later. Monique will make sure you two feel at home. She knows how to get in touch with me."

Tia said, "We cool, see you later. Make sure you check on what we talked about."

Baron smiled. "I'm on it, Carmen." He looked at Monique and said, "Show the ladies around."

Monique smiled. "They're in good hands."

Baron left.

Monique stood up and said, "Let's go get some pizza."

Hours later, inside the Tower Hill apartment, the sounds of Jay-Z's, The Blueprint, CD was coming through the speakers at a respectable volume. Tia was sitting on the sofa smoking weed and nodding her head to the music. Monique sat beside her on her laptop. Vida was in the bedroom sleep...stress and jet lag had her beat.

Monique seemed real cool. She'd taken Vida and Tia out to eat, she took them to Tesco, a somewhat grocery store type joint to get a few things they needed. Then they went to a spot in Chinatown where a friend of hers sold knock off clothes by Gucci, Prada, Louis Vuitton and others for dirt-cheap. Vida and Tia weren't feeling the knockoff shit but they needed some gear. The whole time, Vida didn't say more than a few words. She didn't trust Baron or Monique. She was dealing with them because she had to for the time being. Tia didn't trust them either but she played it real cool in an effort to feel Monique out.

According to the story Monique fed Tia, Monique was twenty-four. She was from the ATL and had moved to the U.K. two years ago to get away from the states because she was tired of the American way of life. She said she was a free spirit and wanted to experience the world. She planned to do so by not living in the same country more than five years for as long as she was able to move from place to place.

Tia wasn't buying one bit of that shit, but she accepted it. After all, she and Vida were living a lie as well. Tia told Monique that she and Vida were from New York and owed some very dangerous people a large amount of money that they couldn't come up with so they decided to disappear. It was the best story she could think of at the time so she rolled with it.

With her eyes on the screen of her laptop, Monique said, "Hey, Carmen, I saw you had Lil Wayne on your iPod, most people from New York don't really like Wayne."

Tia blew weed smoke in the air.

"I can't speak for them. I can only speak for me, I love Lil Wayne, and I don't care where he's from. He could be from London."

Monique laughed at Tia as if what she said was the funniest thing in the world. Tia laughed also. They were high as shit.

Tia passed Monique the blunt and said, "I see you on rap hard."

Monique took a hit of the weed she had provided.

"I love rap…At one time I thought I was going to get a record deal."

Tia laughed hard. "Get the fuck outta here."

"Serious. I had a mix tape out down South in '03 called, *Miss ATL.* The rap thing just didn't work out. I washed my hands of it."

"So what are you into over here?" Tia asked her eyes were slanted and red.

"Straight up," Monique took another puff. "I'm in the drug game."

Tia was surprised that Monique was so straightforward.

Monique saw the surprised look on Tia's face and smiled. "Ecstasy is a big thing. It's a lot of money in it, too."

"I bet it is." Tia didn't feel comfortable talking about drugs with Monique, not at the time anyway.

Monique's cell phone vibrated on the coffee table. She picked it up and answered it.

"I thought you were going to call earlier. It's always something…I can meet you tonight… Thirty minutes… An hour is good… See you then." She ended the call.

Tia said, "Gotta go?"

"Just need to meet this guy. He's been owing me some money for close to a month and keeps bullshitin' me. I hate that."

Couldn't be me, Tia thought, I don't play about my paper.

Monique got up. "I'll be right back, I gotta use the bathroom." She headed down the short hallway.

Tia jumped when the front door opened. Baron smiled. "Take it easy, it's just me." He was carrying a backpack.

Tia said, "What's up?"

He took a seat in the chair beside her and went inside the backpack.

"I got the passports for you." He handed Tia two passports, red ones.

"You move fast." She looked at the pictures inside. Her name was Carol Rucker on the passport; Vida's was Alison Jenkins.

"Those are British passports."

Tia smiled. "So we are British citizens now, huh?"

"Pretty much. Those passports are clean."

Baron went back in the backpack and pulled out two Glocks. "I got the pistols also." He handed Tia the burners.

"That's what I'm talkin' 'bout." Tia held a pistol in both hands. "Now I'm cool."

Baron smiled. "You know what you're doing with those bloody things?"

Tia laughed at the accent. "Hell yeah I know what I'm doin' wit' these joints, but I ain't makin' no noise, I just can't be walkin' around naked."

"Naked?" he smiled.

"Yeah, without no heat."

"Oh," he nodded. "I see."

He handed Tia the backpack.

"A few extra magazines are inside. Be careful, you wouldn't want to get caught with that hardware here."

"I don't plan to either."

Monique walked back into the living room.

"Baron, is something wrong?" The sight of the guns Tia had concerned her.

He said, "No, nothing's wrong. Carmen just wanted some protection."

"Oh," Monique sat back down on the sofa.

Baron said, "I take it that you and Carmen have gotten to know one another."

Monique nodded. "Yeah, we're getting along just fine."

"That's good." Baron stood up to leave "Well, I hate to run but I have business to attend to. Call me if you need anything."

Monique said, "Will do."

Baron left.

Monique looked at Tia and said, "You nice with that pistol?"

Tia laughed.

"Baron just asked me the same thing...Yeah though, I'm nice. Let's hope I never have to get busy over here."

"Wanna rake a ride?"

"I don't care. Let me tell Dawn I'm steppin' out wit' you for a second." Tia said.

News Flash

W alking through her apartment in nothing but her bra and panties, Tera was talking to Paris on the phone about all the drama that had gone down in the streets over the past two days. Shit was off the chain. Four Hell Razor Honeys were shot outside of City Place Mall in Silver Spring, MD no one died but the shooting made the news. Back and forth shootings between young niggas from Congress Park and Saratoga Avenue had shit hot as ever in both hoods. Bodies were dropping left and right. On top of that, news of Lil Rose's murder had everybody close to him shocked and seeking get back.

Paris was crushed when she learned of Lil Rose's murder. She swore she'd kill Styles herself if she could find the nigga. The streets had already found Styles guilty of Lil Rose's murder. Prince George's County already had a warrant for his arrest and had his name and picture in the newspaper.

"The police been here all damn day askin' questions 'bout them killins'. I can see right now it's gon' be a long ass summer. Bodies gon' be droppin' like shit." Tera said.

"You ain't seen nothin' yet. Watch how bad shit get now that Lil Rose got killed. Muhfuckas don't know what they done started." Paris said.

Tera flopped down on her sofa.

"I'ma stay the fuck out the way for a second. It's too much shit goin' on out this bitch." She grabbed the remote and put the TV on BET.

"I feel you on that."

"We need to chill out for a second, Paris, no bullshit."

"I was thinkin' the same thing. Aye…you still ain't heard from Lala?"

"Nah, I don't know what's up wit' her. She won't return my calls." Tera grabbed her lighter and sparked up half a Backwood from earlier. "I think Lala still shook up from that other shit."

"She makin' me worry 'bout her ass. Don't nobody know where the fuck she at, what part of the game is that?"

"I can't call it, Paris." Tera blew smoke in the air and looked over her shoulder. She thought she heard a noise outside her door but brushed it off. The weed had to be playing tricks on her mind.

"Let me get off this phone. I'll be over there in a little while." Paris said.

"See you then." Tera ended the call and finished the rest of the Backwood. Moments later she was bent out from the frame, feeling good.

Her cell phone rang. She grabbed it and looked at the number. It was Marky.

"What's up, boo?" She said.

"Get that ready for me. I'll be there in a few minutes." Marky said. His tone was intense.

"Okay."

"See you in a few." Marky ended the call.

Tera went in her bedroom and got an AK-47 out of her closet that she was holding for Marky. She also grabbed a shoebox full of bullets for the assault rifle. It was no doubt in her mind what was about to go down. Sitting everything on her bed she went back to the living room to wait on Marky.

Loud banging on her front door startled her. The banging stopped for a second and then started again. "Police! Open up!" a voice shouted from the other side of the door.

Tera ran for her bedroom.

"Oh shit." She hissed. She had to hide the AK and the bullets. She heard the front door blast open. The police kicked the door in. Five officers rushed inside. Guns drawn.

The leader of the pack spotted Tera in the bedroom. He shouted, "Don't move! Don't fucking move or I'll shoot!"

Scared to death, Tera put her hands in the air. "Don't shoot." She said. Her whole body was shaking.

Officers rushed her. Slammed her to the floor and slapped handcuffs on her. "You're under arrest for murder."

"I ain't do shit." Tera said.

"Tell it to your lawyer." The officer yanked her to her feet roughly.

Another officer picked up the AK-47 off the bed.

"Damn, this cute little thing is holding some serious firepower."

The officer holding Tera said, "She's one of those Hell Razor Honeys."

Hot steam filled the small bathroom inside Lala's aunt's house on Kennedy street, in Northwest D.C. Lala was crushed about Driver's murder, his murder took a piece of her heart to the after-life. She'd been crying non-stop. Then right after that she heard about Lil Rose getting killed. When would it stop? What was it all for? Lala couldn't take it. She wasn't with the killing, it was too much for her. The whole Hell Razor Honey thing was becoming too much for Lala. That's why she was ducking Paris and Tera. Summer's murder was really haunting her. Lala couldn't close her eyes at night without seeing Summer's murder over and over again.

Coming out of the bathroom in a thick towel, Lala went inside her cousin, Reka's bedroom and got dressed. She threw on a red Prada Sport T-shirt, a pair of blue Louis Vuitton jeans and a pair of black Prada tennis shoes. Looking to her left she grabbed her cell phone and checked her missed calls. Paris and Tera had called a number of times. She sighed. She wasn't in the mood to deal with them at the time. She checked the last text message that Driver sent her.

The text read: *What's up sexy? I been runnin' these streets, takin' care of BI but you stay on my mind. Keep it tight.* ☺

Lala threw the phone on the floor. She wanted to cry but she had no more tears left. "Life's a bitch." She said as she got up and threw on a pair of big frame Prada shades. Growls from her stomach told her it was time to get something to eat so she headed for the carry out.

Stepping outside into the summer sun, Lala wanted to make the trip to the carry out quick. Walking up the busy street, dudes were trying to holla at her sexy-ass left and right but Lala wasn't in the mood at all. Just before she reached the corner of First and Kennedy Street, a black Cadillac Escalade pulled up and stopped a few feet away from her. The tinted window on the passenger's side came down smoothly. The sound of Young Jeezy's, "Soul Survivor", was pumping through the truck's powerful speakers. The music caught Lala's attention. She looked up and saw a girl by the name of Adilah smiling at her behind a slick-ass pair of Gucci shades.

"Lala, pick ya head up, you ain't even see me ride up on you." Adilah said.

Adilah was a Northwest Hell Razor Honey from Kennedy Street. She and the other Hell Razor Honeys from Kennedy Street only hooked up with Paris and the others at go-gos or clubs, other than that, the Kennedy Street Hell Razor Honeys did their own thing uptown.

Lala walked up to the window of the truck as the smell of strong weed hit her in the face. Adilah was riding with a nigga from First and Kennedy by the name of CR.

"I got a thousand things on my mind, Adilah. On the real, I ain't even thinkin' 'bout who ridin' up on me." Lala said.

Chewing gum and popping it, Adilah said, "I heard about your homeboys...That's fucked up."

"Yeah, I'm hurt about that." Lala looked up and down the busy street. Cars were flying by. People were everywhere. Niggas were selling drugs out in the open.

"I heard Tera got locked up for that Summer shit." Adilah said.

"What?!" Lala couldn't believe her ears. Her heart began to race. Fear jumped up and smacked her on the lips.

"Yeah, Tera got locked up earlier today. My phone been jumpin' 'bout that shit there. You ain't know that?"

Lala shook her head. "Nah, my phone been off." She was nervous now. If the police had snatched Tera for Summer's murder then they were sure to be looking for Lala and Paris. I knew this shit was going to happen, Lala thought.

"Look, keep ya eyes open out here in these streets. I'ma catch you later." Adliah said.

"See you later." Lala said.

The Escalade pulled off and made a left on First Street.

Lala stood frozen for a second. She was blown away by the news Adilah had dropped on her. It scared her. She didn't know what to do.

"I told Paris not to do that dumb ass shit! Fuck!" she hissed. Her appetite was gone. She now wanted a damn drink. She hit the liquor store on the corner. Moments later Lala stepped out of the store with a bottle of Remy in a brown paper bag. Her mind was a thousand miles away.

Paris had gotten her and Tera caught up in a bunch of bullshit as far as Lala was concerned.

A white Acura TSX bent the corner and slammed on breaks hard, making the tires scream and drawing the attention of everybody on Kennedy Street. Niggas close by went for their heat. Lala looked up and almost pissed herself. Her eyes grew big with fear. Her mouth dropped open. The bottle of Remy in the brown paper bag crashed to the ground and broke. "Oh my, God!" Lala said out loud as she took off running back up the block. She was in a race for her life.

Automatic gunfire tore through the air with a vengeance. Making people run for cover.

Cee-Cee and Bria were running after Lala spraying compact assault weapons that were spitting rounds of lead by the second.

A bullet slammed into Lala's back just as she got to the door of the liquor store.

"Ahhh…" She yelled as she tumbled into the liquor store and fell on the floor crying out in pain. Bullets came crashing through the front door, making people inside scream and duck for cover.

"Help me, please!" Somebody help me!" Lala screamed as she crawled on the floor.

Police sirens hit the air close by.

Once Lala fell through the front door of the liquor store Cee-Cee and Bria fired a few more shots but then ran back to the car as soon as they heard the police sirens. They took off flying up Kennedy Street.

Inside the liquor store Lala was bleeding badly on the floor. An older woman was kneeling beside her, holding her hand.

"Hold on, child. Help is coming, just hold on. Be strong. Oh, Lord have mercy on this poor child." The older woman said.

Lala was in and out of consciousness, in between life and death. She could feel death pulling her in that everlasting direction as hot lead burned her back. Her whole life flashed before her eyes. "I'm...I'm sorry...I'm sorry for..." Lala tried to say she was sorry for being a part of Summer's murder but she never got it out. Her body went limp.

Hours later, in grave pain, Lala woke up inside a hospital bed hooked up to all kinds of beeping machines. She had tubes running though her nose. She groaned in pain as she tried to look around and figure out where the hell she was. Slowly it all came back to her. She thought she was dead when she heard the shots go off. She felt pleased to be alive. Until she tried to move her arm and found herself handcuffed to the bed.

"What the hell?" She groaned.

Leaning against the wall with his arms folded, a white detective said, "Your under arrest for murder, little lady. You and your Hell Razor Honeys are in a lot of trouble."

Lala laid her head back and closed her eyes. This can't be happening, she thought. It had to be a bad dream, a nightmare.

Pulling a note pad from his shirt pocket along with an ink pen, the detective said, "Before we get into the murder we got you for, let's talk about who shot you."

Lala let out a painful sigh of frustration.

"I know it was the Most Wanted Honeys. Probably came after you for their girl's murder." The detective studied Lala's face. It was expressionless.

The one bullet she'd taken to the back had her feeling like she'd been in a terrible car crash.

Lala said, "I don't know shit. I don't know who shot me and I don't know shit 'bout no murder."

The detective shook his head. "Let me guess, you're down with the 'stop snitching' movement, or the whole 'death before dishonor' thing. That's all bullshit. When your pretty young ass is sitting in a federal prison for life you won't be so in love with those codes then."

Lala sighed and rolled her eyes. "If I'm under arrest you can talk that shit to my lawyer."

Inside a Temple Hills, MD hotel room Styles sat on the bed drinking Hennessy from the bottle as he watched BET. They were doing a special on Lil Kim. It was a hot topic in the hip-hop circles that Lil' Kim kept her mouth shut when questioned by the feds about a 2001 gunfight outside of New York's radio station, Hot 97. Lil Kim kept it gangsta and refused to identify D-Roc and C-Gutta. For sticking to the code, Lil Kim was to lay down a year and a day. Not bad at all, considering her honor remained intact.

Styles nodded his head and said, "That's right, baby girl, don't tell them crackas shit." He took another swig of Hennessy.

Sitting the bottle on the floor, he got up and went to the window and looked down at the dark parking lot. Samara had left the hotel twenty minutes ago to meet Styles's man, Eyes, to get some money for him. On the run for murder, Styles was laying low until he could get out of the D.C. area. He couldn't believe the police had a warrant out on him so fast for Lil Rose's murder. The news said a witness took pictures of the shooting and the tag number of Styles' Lexus with a camera phone and gave the pictures to police. Styles was blown away when he saw that on the news.

Walking back to the bed Styles flopped down on it and stretched out, putting his arms behind his head. He let out a stressful sigh. He didn't have enough money to make it on the run. He was hoping his man, Eyes, could throw him a few thousand. That would help out, it could get him down South somewhere. He could find a way to make a few moves once he was there.

About ten minutes later there was a sound outside the door. Styles jumped up and grabbed a 21-shot Glock and rushed to the door.

The door opened and Styles relaxed. It was Samara.

Shutting the door behind her, she said, "Eyes gave me five thousand, and Creek gave me five-thousand." She handed Styles two brown paper bags.

He looked inside the bags and nodded. This should hold a nigga for a second, he thought. He hugged Samara and kissed her on the forehead. "Thanks, boo."

Samara made a frustrated sound. She was stressed out. First she had to deal with Vida and Tia's situation, now she had to deal with the shit Styles was caught up in.

Styles could read her mind by the look on her beautiful face.

"I already know what's on your mind, boo. I wish it was somethin' I could do to make this shit right but I gotta play the cards I was dealt."

"I can't take it, Styles. I love you. I really do, but I can't get caught up in this shit. I've worked too hard to get my life together. I...I just can't...I mean-"

Styles kissed her and gave her his tongue, hugging her tightly. Showing he had love for her too, he pulled her closely giving her an understanding look.

"I understand, boo. The last thing I'd ever want to do is fuck up your life. I love you too much for that, Sam."

Her eyes got watery. She didn't want to lose Styles. However, she couldn't go on the run with him. That was out.

She said, "I need to go, Styles. The longer I stay here wit' you the harder it gets to say goodbye."

"Let me make love to you one more time, boo. I don't know when I'll see you again, Sam."

He kissed her again, dropped the brown paper bags on the carpeted floor and moved Samara to the bed. He sat his Glock on the nightstand and laid her on the bed. Then he climbed on top of her and kissed her again. Softly, he bit her bottom lip and she moaned.

"I'll always love you, Sam. Always, boo."

"I don't want to lose you, Styles."

"I'll find a way to fix this, boo." Styles smoothly undressed Samara then did the same to himself.

Styles eased inside her and made her moan as she wrapped her legs around him. Her hands rubbed up and down his back. He sucked her neck as he began to long-stroke her wetness at a nice pace.

She moaned, "I love you, Styles, I love you so much." She moved her hips to the pace of his long, deep strokes. With every satisfying stroke she felt her walls stretching wider.

"Oh, God, I love you…. Ahhh… I love you so much."

"Styles…Styles…Styles. Oh, God, Styles, don't stop…Just don't." She closed her eyes and bit her bottom lip, moving her hips to his deep penetration.

He slid his big hands under her soft ass and gripped it with passion as he dug inside her. With every stroke he pulled her ass to him, trying to get deeper inside her. She moaned deeply and used her legs to pull him deeper inside her.

"I need you so bad, Styles." She moaned. Her nails dug into his back.

"Ah," he groaned from the sting of her nails. He dug inside her with more force.

"Uh, uh, uh, uh, yeah, fuck me…Fuck me like that…Just like that."

Styles pulled out.

"No, don't stop. Don't stop." She cried.

"Turn over." Styles turned her over on her hands and knees. He had her pretty brown ass up in the air. Grabbing her by her waist he dug back inside her.

"Oh yes, oh God, yes!"

Rain began to fall.

Outside of Styles' hotel door two gunmen in ski masks were paying close attention to what was going on inside. One had an Uzi machine gun with a silencer on it. The other had a .32 automatic with a silencer on it.

Uzi in hand, with his ear to the door, Marky looked at Jazz and whispered, "I'ma kick the door open and we gon' go in bussin', moe."

Jazz was 17 years old, he was Driver's right-hand man. He and Marky had been stalking Styles since Lil Rose was murdered. They'd spotted Samara and followed her to the hotel.

Jazz had a concerned look in his eyes. He whispered, "What about Sam, moe?"

"She fuckin' the nigga that smashed Rose. She gon' get it too, besides that, we ain't leavin' no witnesses."

Jazz took a deep breath. He was all for killing Styles but Samara was cool. She was from the hood. Jazz didn't want to kill her.

Marky could tell Jazz was questioning Samara's fate. Marky whispered, "We gotta do it, moe. Come on, let's get it over wit'. I'm soakin' wet already."

"Let's rock then." Jazz said, gripping his pistol tightly.

With speed and force, Marky kicked the hotel door open.

Styles pushed Samara off the bed and dove for his Glock as the first silenced shots went off.

Jazz hit Styles in the back five times. Samara screamed at the top of her lungs, until Marky ran up on her and sprayed her in the face and chest with the Uzi. Brains and blood stained the brown carpet.

Jazz gave Styles the rest of his clip to the head with the quickness, blowing brains all over the place.

Marky said, "let's roll, let's roll!" He headed for the door, kicking one of the brown paper bags. Money spilled out of it. Quickly, he snatched up both paper bags full of cash.

Jazz grabbed Styles' Glock and jogged behind Marky, leaving death inside the hotel room.

New Leads

Behind his desk in the FBI's Washington, D.C. field office, Agent Brewer drank his second cup of coffee as he read the newspaper. The Metro section of the *Washington Post* had an article covering the recent spike in murders in the D.C. area and what police were trying to do about it. A number of the murders had occurred in Prince George's County, MD. After the gruesome discovery of Samara and Styles' bodies in a Temple Hills hotel, the chief of police released a strong statement:

"The level of violence that's occurring on the streets of Prince George's County is unacceptable and I will not tolerate this type of violence. Some arrests have already been made. Two members of the girl gang, the Hell Razor Honeys, are in custody and are being charged with first-degree murder. Another member of the gang, Paris Wright, is still being sought. Our police department is prepared and we are going to set the tone once again on the streets of Prince George's County."

Brewer shook his head. These little Hell Razor Honeys are out of control, he thought. Here it was he and his partner were after Vida and Tia for a number of murders including the murder of law enforcement— and another group of Hell Razor Honeys were still raising hell in the streets. "What the hell is the world coming to?" Brewer said to himself.

So far, the only leads the FBI had on Vida and Tia were pointing toward Philly and New York. Tips were still coming in but nothing strong enough to move on. Nevertheless, the FBI refused to let up on Vida and Tia.

Agent Arnold walked up with a folder in his hand and a smug look on his face. He dropped the folder on the desk for Brewer to see.

"Take a look inside, buddy."

Brewer looked inside the folder and shook his head.

"Where the hell did this come from?"

"New York. Major Crimes busted an operation that sells fake IDs and passports…Some Nigerians."

Brewer smiled. "Well I'll be damned." He couldn't believe how easy it was to get a lead on Vida and Tia.

"Can you believe how this shit just fell right into our hands?" Arnold said.

"Brewer nodded. "We need to get on top of this right now."

"I agree." Arnold said.

Paris pulled into the dark parking lot behind her apartment building and parked in the back. She cut the car off and killed the lights. Knowing that the police were after her she should have been far away from Saratoga Avenue but in her present frame of mind Paris didn't give a fuck about anything. She was still dealing with the murder of Lil Rose when she found out that her cousin, Samara, had been murdered along with Styles. She didn't give a fuck about Styles, he was an anything-ass nigga to Paris but Samara was her flesh and blood. She was hurt about Samara's murder. Tears were not her style but she was unable to control them when she got the call about Sam. Death came at any given time.

The stakes were high all the way around the board. Paris knew that the first-degree murder charge that was waiting for her was nothing to take lightly. She really didn't know what to do to get herself out of the shit she'd gotten into. With Tera and Lala already in jail, Paris knew that she was the last bitch standing. That meant it was her job to help Tera and Lala in any way possible. From the sidelines she'd paid close attention to the way Vida, Tia and Ice used to deal with shit in the streets, she had a game plan mapped out.

The young Jeezy ringtone on her cell phone grabbed her attention. Paris looked at the caller ID. It was her girl, Capri, a Forestville Maryland Hell Razor Honey. Capri was also a cousin of Tera's.

Paris answered, "What's up, Capri?"

"I spoke to Tera. She ain't say much over the phone but I'ma go see her tomorrow. I should be able to let you know more then." Capri said with her baby voice.

"Good. Did you check on Lala?"

"Yeah, talked to her mother. She's okay, they still got her in the hospital but they gon' be movin' her to the jail in a few days until they turn her over to Maryland."

"Okay," Paris nodded. Coming across the dark parking lot was just who she was looking for. She pulled a

.380 from her Gucci bag and cocked it. "I gotta take care of somethin', Capri. Stay on top of that for me, boo."

"No problem, you know I got that. I'm 'bout to head out for the night, me and my girls gon' run down on some of them Most Wanted bitches."

Paris said, "That's right, let them bitches know Hell Razor ain't to be fucked wit'." She ended the call and dropped the phone on the seat as she got out of the car.

"Aye, Mechanic, let me holla at you real quick." Paris approached Mechanic with her hands behind her back. Pistol gripped tight.

Aside from Paris and Mechanic, the dark parking lot was empty.

"What's up, Paris? What the hell you doin' out here? Don't you know the police is lookin' for you? Your ass is hot, you need to be layin' low somewhere, baby girl." Mechanic looked like he was geekin' for some coke, gritting his teeth and shit.

Looking around the parking lot, Paris said, "Yeah I know I'm hot right now but I'm fucked up 'bout Lil Rose and Samara. I'm trying to find out who the fuck would kill them. You heard anything about who killed Lil Rose?"

"Nah," Mechanic looked over his shoulder. When he looked back at Paris he saw a pistol in his face.

"Sorry 'bout this." Paris said.

Pop! Pop! Pop!

Shots to the face. Mechanic hit the ground.

Paris looked down at him with cold eyes.

Pop! Pop! Two more to the head.

Can't leave no loose ends, Paris thought as she walked back to the stolen car she was pushing.

In front of Ben's Chili Bowl a group of Most Wanted Honies gathered around a blue BMW 745i that had go-go music pumping through the speakers. There were a number of people outside on U Street, in Northwest D.C.

A pretty dark-skinned girl by the name of Rachel seemed to be doing all the talking. She and the girls with her had caught a group of Hell Razor Honeys on Georgia Avenue and gave them the business, stabbing three of them. A little more than an hour had passed since then.

Sipping on a Pepsi, Rachel said, "Them Hell Razor bitches don't know what they done started."

"They gon' find out, real quick." Said another girl named Maria. She had put some serious knife work in on the Hell Razor Honeys on Georgia Avenue.

A few other girls made comments about the Hell Razor Honeys. They were feeling themselves in a major way.

"I heard somebody punished that fake-ass bitch, Lala up on Kennedy Street." Rachel said.

"They shoulda killed her ass for that shit they did to Summer." Maria said.

All the Most Wanted Honies were fucked up about Summer's murder.

A girl by the name of Toni added, "Somebody need to catch that bitch Paris and put a bullet in her ass. She done got beside her damn self."

"Oh, she gon' get hers." Maria said.

Rachel agreed, "Believe that."

Moments later a white Acura TSX pulled up and parked behind the blue BMW. Cee-Cee and Bria stepped on the scene dressed to impress, as if they were going out to party. They spread love and spoke to the other Most Wanted Honies.

"Where the hell y'all goin'?" Rachel asked.

"Jay-Z goin' be down the H20. We gon' slide through. We might even run into some of them Hell Razor bitches." Cee-Cee said.

"We stabbed the shit out them bitches." Toni said.

Cee-Cee smiled. "That's right, keep puttin' that work in."

As the Most Wanted Honies continued to congregate in front of Ben's, a brown Crown Vic bent the corner with five heads inside. The Crown Vic slowed and stopped. Doors flew open. All of the Most Wanted Honies took off running in different directions. Jump-out cops in bullet-proof vest, jeans and tennis shoes gave chase with their Glocks drawn.

Cee-Cee made it to Florida Avenue before a skinny, white cop tackled her. On the ground, Cee-Cee screamed, "Get the fuck off me!" She struggled.

The cops roughly slapped handcuffs on Cee-Cee. "You're under arrest young lady."

Not far away, on V Street by the gas station, Bria was arrested as well.

The U.K.

I t was raining in London.
Vida stood at the window looking at the gray skies. She and Tia had been in London for a week now. Vida's stress level was down to a manageable degree at this time. To a certain extent she felt like they had succeeded in disappearing but common sense told her that life would never be normal again. She accepted her reality.

Looking at the rainfall reminded her of the tears she had shed for those she loved and held dear in her heart. Not a day went by that she didn't mourn for her husband, Moe-Moe and her girl Bloody. Real talk, all she had left in life was Tia, literally.

Taking a deep breath, Vida sat on the sofa and turned her attention back to the TV. She was watching the movie, "Paid in Full", on DVD. Vida spent most of her time, so far, watching DVD's. Monique brought a bunch of American DVDs for Vida and Tia to watch.

"Aye, Vee," Tia came into the living room carrying Monique's laptop. "Look at this shit." She sat right beside Vida.

Vida looked at the screen. Tia was checking out the *Washington Post* website. There was an article with a headline that read: **Hell Razor Honeys Still a Threat**.

The article detailed all the violence over the past week and blamed it all on Hell Razor and Most Wanted. The murders of Driver, Lil Rose, Summer, Samara, and Styles were all attributed to the beef between the two "girl gangs" as the Post put it. Tera and Lala were both being held in PG County on first-degree murder charges. Paris, who was being called the new leader of the Hell Razor Honeys was still on the run for murder. Cee-Cee and Bria were being held in Montgomery County, MD for the shooting of four Hell Razor Honeys. The end of the article recapped all the events that had Vida and Tia on the run.

Vida sighed and shook her head. "Got-damn, they goin' crazy back home. All those damn murders in a few days?"

Tia shrugged. "Drama City. I'm jive fucked up 'bout Lil Rose and Sam, though."

Vida nodded, "Yeah me too, I wonder what that's all about there."

"Ain't no tellin', Vee." Tia clicked to a few other articles that were talking about the drama in D.C.

"Paris done lost her mind." Vida said.

"You know she always wanted to carry shit like we used to back in the day when Tec and Ice was alive."

"Yeah, I know." Vida reflected for a second on their past. They had started the Hell Razor Honeys, so in a way they were responsible for the madness in the D.C. streets that was connected to the young Hell Razor Honeys. "So much has changed so fast, Tee."

Tia nodded, "Yeah, I know...I woulda never thought we'd be way over here in London, on the run. But hey-"

she shrugged, "what can we do besides roll wit' the punches?"

"I feel you. I already made my mind up that we goin' just make the best of the situation. It's whatever. Like you said, ain't no turnin' back now."

Tia agreed by nodding and raising her eyebrows. "You got that right. I was thinkin'…It ain't like we sittin' on millions, so the money we got only gon' last but so long. We gon' have to make some moves sooner or later. You know that right?"

Vida sighed. "Yeah, I know, but I've been tryin' not to think about that, for real."

"We gotta think about it, Vee. We can't stay up in this safe house forever. We gotta get out and get our feet wet, find out who's who and what's what. In our position we can't stay in one spot too long, and we gon' need paper to keep movin' around, boo."

"What you got in mind, Tee?"

"I been talkin' to Monique, gettin' a feel for what she got goin' on and I think I can talk her into lettin' us in on her thing. Shit, we got some cash. The way she put it, the "E" pills be pumpin' like shit in the clubs over here. It's somethin' to think about, Vee, on everything."

Vida rubbed her temple with her right hand. It wasn't like they had a lot of options, on the run, all the way in London.

Tia knew Vida was weighing the odds. She said, "It ain't like we can live the square life, Vee. We goin' have to get in where we fit in, boo."

Vida made sounds of frustration. "I got too much on my mind right now to really give it some serious thought but go ahead and check it all out. If it sounds good to you, make the move."

Tia nodded. "Cool, I'll holla at Monique when she get back. We'll see what's good."

Placing her hand on the Glock that sat beside her, Vida said, "Whatever you do, keep in mind that we don't need attention. No heat at all, Tia."

Tia winked at Vida. "I got this."

"Countless reporters gathered outside of the L.A. court house as No Draws, her lawyer and Daddieo stepped out into the beautiful summer afternoon. Questions came from all directions. Cameras snapped left and right. No Draws smiled and answered a few questions as she made her way through the crowd to a waiting Benz limo.

A reporter yelled, "What's next for you?!"

No Draws looked over her shoulder with a smile and said, "The sky's the limit."

Once they made it to the limo, No Draws gave her lawyer a hug and a kiss on the cheek. Looking into his eyes she said, "Lawrence, you're the best lawyer money can buy. I don't know what I would have done without you. I'll be by your office in a few days."

Lawrence smiled. "See you then."

No Draws waved to the reporters and stepped inside the limo. Daddieo stepped in behind her and shut the door. The limo pulled off.

Sitting beside No Draws with his arm around her, Daddieo just looked at her for a while, taking in her beauty for a moment. He had missed her for the few months she'd spent in jail.

No Draws smiled. "You missed me?"

"You know it."

She kissed his lips. "Well I'm back and we gon' do big things."

Daddieo nodded. "Sounds good to me, I got a few things lined up for you too, once you ready."

"I'm always ready. I'm ready more than ever now. However, I do have one mission I need to attend to."

Daddieo raised his eyebrows.

"I want you to destroy Marky Miles." No Draws had a serious look on her face.

Daddieo smiled and shook his head. "You just got out, Michelle."

"I know, but I'm not going to do anything crazy. I just want to expose him for bein' the dick lovin' gump that he is."

Daddieo laughed. "You are mean as shit."

"He tried to cross me, I don't play that snake shit." No Draws shook her head. "I'ma show his ass."

Changing the subject, Daddieo said, "You heard about Vida and Tia?"

"Nah, what about them bitches?" No Draws had no love for her old friends.

Daddieo put No Draws on point about Vida and Tia. He'd been in New York two days ago and learned about the girl's situation. Unlike No Draws, Daddieo still had love for Vida, no matter what had happened between them in the past.

"Fuck them bitches, they ain't never been shit anyway." No Draws waved her hand.

Daddieo shook his head with a smirk on his face.

No Draws smiled at Daddieo and said, "Come here, boo, let me please you. I've missed you so much."

She went straight for his pants, pulling his manhood out and stroking it a few times as she looked into his eyes. Her eyes told him how bad she wanted to suck him off. Her soft hand stroked him to a strong erection. She loved the way his dick grew in her hand. She leaned over and took him in her mouth, pleasing him. His eyes closed, he leaned his head back and rubbed his left hand through her hair. With her hands and her mouth, No Draws went to work, giving Daddieo serious pleasure. Wet sounds filled the back of the limo. Although the AC was on, the heat inside the limo was at an all time high. No Draws took her mouth off of him for a second but continued to stroke him with her hand.

Looking up at him, she said, "I missed this big dick so much, Daddieo."

He moaned from her touch and pushed her head back down on his dick.

"Ahhh, baby, I love the way you suck this dick." He moved his hips upward, sliding deeper into her throat.

No Draws' head began to go up and down on his dick with more and more passion as she got into the act. She loved the way he tasted. His pre-cum coated the inside of her hungry mouth. She knew he was close to cumming. She looked forward to his thick cream pouring into her mouth and sliding down her throat. As she sucked his dick her pussy grew wetter by the second, her clit grew hard and throbbed. She would need to be fucked good and hard when she was done pleasing him orally.

Daddieo moaned, "I'm 'bout to cum...Ahhh." His body tensed up and he held her head in place as he exploded in her mouth. "Ahhhh.... Damn, I missed you girl."

No Draws swallowed all that he released into her mouth.

Taking a deep breath, Daddieo said, "I can't get enough of you, baby."

No Draws licked her lips and smiled.

"It's me and you against the world from here on out, daddy." She said.

He smiled as she continued to stroke his dick with her soft hand.

"We gon' take Hollywood by storm this go 'round...We gon' have more money than we can spend in two lifetimes." She said.

Daddieo smiled.

"I love the sound of that, me and you against the world."

Marky was behind the wheel of a black Caprice Classic headed south on I-95 just as the sun set, Young Jeezy was pumping through the speakers. Marky needed the thug motivation. With a .40 caliber Ruger on his lap,

Marky puffed on a weed packed Backwood. His mind was racing at top speed with thoughts of all that was going on in the D.C. streets. Shit would never be the same without his right-hand man, Lil Rose. With Styles dead there was nothing else to do about Lil Rose's murder. The hood was on fire with police pressure and shoot-outs so Marky decided to head south for a while. He had peoples in the ATL.

Hitting his little man, Jazz off with $5,000 and a brick of coke, Marky hit the road with $15,000 and two bricks. He was sure he could make some moves in A-Town.

Looking to his right, Marky passed Paris the Backwood and said, "You rolled that jive 'aight."

"Whatever." She rolled her eyes and hit the 'J'.

Marky didn't feel good about what he'd done to Samara, but justified it in his heart by reminding himself that Samara was sleeping with the other side. Samara knew what she was doing by fucking with Styles, Marky told himself, and for fucking with Styles she deserved everything she got. Nevertheless, Marky would never be able to get Paris to understand such a thing nor would he try. He had love for Paris and that was the only reason he agreed to let her roll with him to Atlanta. She stressed to him how hot it was for her in the D.C. area with the law on her back for the first-degree murder charge. The police had run up in a number of spots looking for her. Marky couldn't leave her behind, his heart wouldn't let him. So off to Atlanta they were.

Blowing smoke in the air, Paris said, "It's fucked up we ain't get to go to none of them funerals."

They couldn't make it to the funeral of Driver, Lil Rose, or Samara.

"Yeah, I'm fucked up 'bout that there." Marky said.

She passed the Backwood back to Marky.

He took a hit and said, "I'm still fucked up somebody got to Styles' anything-ass before me. I wanted to punish his ass myself for Driver and Lil Rose." He blew smoke out the left side of his mouth.

"I'm so hurt that Sam got caught up wit' that nigga. I know whoever killed Sam was after Styles." Paris shook her head, feeling sorry for what happened to her cousin, Samara.

Marky passed her the Backwood and said, "Yeah, Sam caught a bad one." He spoke with a straight face and a calm voice, showing no sign that he had murdered Samara.

"I don't know what Sam seen in that nigga Styles anyway. Fuckin' wit' his ass, now she dead." Paris said as she shook her head and took a long pull on the Backwood.

Marky wanted to change the subject, he didn't feel comfortable talking about Samara.

"I wonder how that shit goin' play out wit' Tera and Lala…I wish it was something I could do to help them out." He said.

"Yeah me too but I'm too hot in the city."

"I feel you." Marky said as they crossed the state line into North Carolina.

"I got Tera's cousin on top of shit for me though. I'm stayin' in contact wit' her to keep up wit' what's goin' on wit' Tera and Lala."

231

"Aye," Marky cut his eyes at Paris. "You heard what happened to Mechanic?"

Blowing a thick cloud of smoke into the air, Paris said, "Yeah, I heard somebody shot him."

"Yeah, I wonder what the fuck that was all about...Niggas killin' pipe heads and shit now. Them young niggas from Congress Park might've came through and couldn't find nobody else to shoot at."

Paris shrugged. "You know how shit is, ain't no tellin'."

She had her secret and Marky had his...neither would never share their secret to the other.

Last Chance

Margarita in her hand, Vida sat across from Tia at their table in a London restaurant called Banner's, on Park road. The restaurant was a smooth joint with top of the line service and a variety of food in the Crouch End area of London. Monique had taken Vida and Tia out to eat. She wanted to spend more time with Vida and Tia since she'd agreed to let them in on her Ecstasy hustle. After a little thought, and some coaxing on Tia's part, Monique was interested in the "expansion" idea Tia was pushing.

Sipping red wine, Monique said, "I can turn your twenty-thousand pounds into sixty-thousand in no time. I'll just put it all together with what I'm putting up. It'll be a nice partnership. I like the idea. I only have one question."

Vida raised her eyebrows. "And what's that?"

"How do we really know we can trust each other?" Monique said.

Tia laughed a little. A Glock was in her Gucci bag.

Vida smiled.

"Trust has to start somewhere, let's just hope we all have good intentions." Tia said.

233

Monique sipped the last of her red wine and said, "So there it is, we're in it to win it."

Tia nodded with a smile.

"So, uh, who's your competition?" Vida asked. "When it's a lot of money involved it's gotta be competition."

"Right now, I'm not running into any trouble. I'm only dealing with the club scene. There are some guys from Brixton that have a strong hold on the street level dealing but I don't have an interest in that."

Vida nodded.

"Well, I guess it ain't no toes to step on then, right?" Tia questioned.

"Ecstasy is a beautiful thing here, you'll see." Monique assured.

It's always toes to step on, Vida thought, but she didn't voice her thought. She knew she and Tia had to find a way to make some money and the Ecstasy move seemed to be the best option at the time.

"On another note," Monique said, "I've found a nice flat for you two to rent. It's in a nice area in Wimbledon. I'll take you to check it out."

"We can go check that out after we hit you off wit' our share of the money for you to cop wit'." Tia said.

Monique nodded. "Let's get that out the way before it gets dark."

They all left Banners.

Outside of Banners, cars cruised up and down the two-lane road. The mid day heat was in full effect but people were still out and about. Out of the blue a tall light skinned dude with cornrows stepped to Monique. He was in jean shorts and a white T-shirt.

"Monique!" He spoke loudly. "Why don't you return my bloody calls?!"

Monique looked shocked, almost afraid. She took a step back from the light-skinned guy. Vida and Tia grew very alert. They stood by Monique's side, Vida to the right and Tia to the left.

"Claude… I told you I want you to leave me alone. Are you stalking me or some shit?!" Monique said, stammering.

Vida sighed at the attention the scene was drawing. Tia looked around and slipped her hand inside her Gucci bag.

"It's Baron isn't it? You're seeing that bloody wanker, aren't you?" Claude said.

"None of your business, motherfucker!" Monique tried to hurry by Claude. He grabbed her arm with a firm grip.

"Get the fuck off me!" Monique tried to snatch her arm away but his grip was too firm.

Claude hissed, "You are going to talk to me."

Vida spoke up. "Aye! Aye! Aye! Main man, you need to ease up." Her eyes were dead serious.

"Who the fuck is this bloody-" Claude's words got stuck in his throat when he saw Tia ease the Glock out of her Gucci bag.

"Let her go, nigga." Tia demanded.

235

Claude removed his hand off of Monique. Fear filled his eyes as he looked from Tia's eyes to the Glock at her side.

Monique stepped beside Vida and was surprised that Tia pulled out a pistol on a busy London street.

"Step off, slim, get on 'bout your business. I'm only gon' tell you once." Tia said.

Claude rushed across the street, barely being hit by a car, and jumped on a BMW motorcycle. Although he looked afraid his eyes were hateful.

"Bitch, bloody bitch." He mumbled as he put on his helmet and started the engine. Giving Monique one last mean glare he pulled off.

Tia slid the Glock back inside her Gucci bag. She looked around to see who was looking at her. A few eyes were pierced on her.

Vida looked around and said, "Let's go."

They rushed to Monique's red Audi and got out of the area. Monique kept her eyes on the road and said, "Carmen, you handled that so well, you and Dawn. Thank you both so much." Monique was impressed with the way Vida and Tia took control.

Vida looked out the window and said nothing for a moment.

Tia, sitting in the back said, "Who the hell was that bamma ass nigga?"

Monique sighed. "I used to go out with Claude, but he wanted too much. I'm not looking for a husband, or a father for that matter. He got too damn controlling. I ain't have time for that shit. But, now this asshole keeps popping up on me in the damnedest of places."

"I thought I was goin' have to smoke his ass, dumb ass nigga." Tia said rolling her eyes.

"I'm glad you didn't let his ass have it." Vida said before looking at Monique. "You feel safe wit' that nigga sweatin' you like that? He was kinda aggressive." She asked.

"Kinda?" Tia huffed. "That nigga put his hands on you...Shhhhiiidddd, I don't play that shit there."

"Claude wouldn't hurt me, he just can't handle rejection. He'll get the idea."

"Sometimes you gots to be real firm wit' niggas so they get the drift." Vida said.

"I'll deal with Claude, he'll cool off." Monique said.

Changing the subject, Monique turned the conversation back to moving Ecstasy. She and her new friends talked about making money all the way back to the Tower Hill apartment.

A week later Vida and Tia sat in the living room of the Wimbledon flat that they were now renting, thanks to Monique. At the moment there was only a modest sofa and a nice TV in the living room. On the floor they counted the money that Monique had flipped for them.

Like it was nothing, Monique turned their twenty thousand pounds into sixty thousand, just as she said she would.

Wrapping a rubber band around a stack of bills, Vida said, "Monique really knows what she'd doin'."

"I'm hip." Tia nodded. "We could stack a lotta paper on the sneak tip fuckin' wit' her. We don't even gotta play the front line."

"Yeah, I know...that jive been on my mind. Ain't nothin' free... It's a catch to everything, Tee."

Tia laughed. "That's why I love you, Vee."

"What?" Vida raised her eyebrows.

"You always a few steps ahead of the game." Tia smiled and shook her head.

"Shit, it's chess, not checkers, boo." Vida stretched and yawned.

"Monique seems like she's glad to have two girlfriends from the states. I think she knows we got some serious troubles back home and she wants to help us out."

"Sounds good but just remember that we can't trust nobody for real."

"Vee, I'm hip. You know that."

Vida nodded. "I know you hip. Anyway...I think we can stack enough paper to take care of business."

"No doubt. Right now Monique gon' be our meal ticket." Tia said seriously. "We gon' keep her close."

Vida stuffed all the money in a gym bag and took it to the bedroom. She returned and said, "When's Monique comin' over?"

Looking out the front window, Tia said, "Half hour. She said she want us to ride wit' her to drop the re-up money off. I guess she feels safer havin' us wit' her while she carryin' that much paper."

"I can dig that." Vida flopped down on the sofa. She sighed, still carrying the weight of the world on her shoulders. Looking at Tia, Vida said, "Aye, Tee, you's a real soldier, you know that?"

"Why you say that, Vee?" Tia took a seat on the sofa.

"You don't let shit bother you. All the shit we been through in the past few weeks and you ain't lost a step. I'm still fucked up. I can't get over the fact that everything went down like it did."

Tia gave an understanding nod. "Vee, I'm fucked up still, but I know we all we got at this point and we gotta do whatever it takes to survive."

"Yeah, you got that right." Vida said.

A knock at the door got their attention.

Tia headed for the door. "Must be Monique."

The FBI was in London, after Vida and Tia. Agents Brewer and Arnold were working in conjunction with the British fugitive task force. Leads from New York had led them to Baron who was snatched up as he left a club. He was whisked off to an undisclosed location where he was questioned about Vida and Tia. He was shown pictures of them and told they were wanted in the U.S. for a number of murders.

Baron told them he knew nothing about Vida and Tia.

"Bullshit! Bloody bullshit!" A British agent shouted into Baron's face, leaning across the metal table in the tiny, smoke-filled room.

Baron sat on the other side in handcuffs. The two FBI agents stood against the wall behind the British agent.

In his British accent, Baron said, "I'll tell you again, I know nothing about these women you are looking for."

"We are about to raid your bloody flat and your place of business. We know you helped to get these fugitives into the U.K...Your friends in the U.S. have already informed us."

That got Baron's attention. The agent wasn't supposed to know anything about the U.S. operation. Someone in the States had to be talking to the FBI.

The British agent said, "All we want are the girls. We want them out of this country. If you give up the girls you walk free."

Baron's mind began to race.

Agents Brewer and Arnold were all ears.

"What's it going to be, mate?" The British agent pressed Baron.

Baron sighed. He was sweating like he was under the baking sun.

"Okay, I can give you the girls."

The British agent looked back and the American FBI agents and smiled.

Tia opened the door and saw Monique with her head down wearing a pair of Prada shades even though it was dark outside.

"What's up, Monique?" Tia said letting Monique inside. "What's wit' the shades, boo?"

"I need a gun." Monique said.

Vida became very alert. "For what?" She asked.

Monique pulled off her shades. She had a mean black eye.

"Damn," Tia said, taking a close look at her eye. "What the fuck happened to you?"

Vida stood up to get a good look at Monique as well.

"Claude…He came to my apartment."

Monique shook her head. "I shoulda never opened the damn door."

Vida said, "He put his hands on you?"

Monique nodded her head. "He was in a rage, yelling and screaming."

Tia shook her head.

"I told his ass to leave and he hit me." Monique continued.

Tia said, "Oh fuck that, I don't play that shit. His ass would've been full of that hot shit, believe that."

"So you wanna gun now? You sure?" Vida questioned.

"Hell yeah!" Monique shot back.

Vida sighed. "Where the nigga at?"

"I'm sure he's at home by now, wondering if I'm going to call the cops. But fuck that. I want to put a bullet in his ass." Monique stated.

Vida looked at Tia for a second.

Tia shrugged. "She wanna bus' the nigga let her bus' the nigga."

Vida looked at Monique and asked, "You know what you doin'?"

"If you're askin' if I ever shot somebody before, no."

"Shit, it's a first time for everything. Let a nigga put his hands on me, bullets gon' fly." Tia said.

"Fuck it, we got your back. Come on. Let's go see the nigga." Vida said.

Monique knocked on the door of Claude's apartment with a nervous feeling in her gut.

Vida and Tia stood to the left and right of Monique, out of peephole range. They had their Glocks out, at their side.

Looking up and down the hallway, Vida said, "You sure the nigga will open the door?" They'd been outside for a few minutes.

Monique said, "If he was here I'm sure he'd open the door." She then pulled out her cell phone and called Claude. He answered on the first ring. "I need to see you, Claude." Monique said, looking at Vida and Tia.

"Monique, I'm so sorry about how I acted. I never meant for things to get out of hand. Please-"

"Where are you, Claude?" Monique cut him off.

"I needed a drink."

"When are you coming home?"

"I'll be home in about an hour." Claude said.

"We need to talk. Call me when you get home." Monique ended the call. Looking at Vida and Tia she said, "He'll be home in an hour or so. We can come back."

All three of them left the building and got back into Monique's car. As soon as they got in Monique's car Monique's cell phone rang. It was Baron. She answered.

"Where have you been? I have been calling you over and over again." She asked him.

"I've been on top of a few things and my phone was in the car. Where are you?" He lied.

"Out with Dawn and Carmen."

"I need to see them, it's very important. Meet me at the Tower Hill apartment." Baron ended the call.

"What's up?" Vida said.

"Baron said he needs to see you and Carmen. Said it's important." Monique started the car and pulled into traffic.

"Baron ain't say what was up?" Tia asked.

"No, just said it was important." Monique said.

There was light foot traffic on the street when Monique parked across the street from the hotel. Darkness was broken by the streetlights.

Monique cut the car off.

"Maybe I should get Baron to deal with Claude for me...Claude respects Baron."

Tia shrugged. "That's on you, home girl."

All three of them stepped out of the car and headed for the building.

Something felt funny and out of place to Tia. She stopped and looked around, Vida picked up on Tia's vibe and looked around as well.

Monique pulled a sensor key from her pocket and waved it in front of the sensor pad, opening the glass door. She looked back at Vida and Tia as she held the door open and picked up on their vibe.

"What's wrong?" She looked around the street as well and to her, everything seemed normal. A few cars and mopads cruised up and down.

"Somethin' ain't right…" Tia said. She looked down the street toward Trinity Square and then in the other direction. She looked across the street at the hotel and eyed people that were going in and out. Two white dudes were looking right in her face.

Vida eased closer to the door as she looked at all the parked cars on the side of the street closest to her. "Yeah something is out of place."

"What are you two talking about? I don't see-" Monique froze in mid statement.

Car doors flew open. Armed agents seemed to come from every direction screaming with British accents, "Fugitive Task Force! Get on the ground!"

"Shit!" Tia pulled her Glock instantly and let off rounds hitting an agent in the face from about ten-feet away. She dropped the agent.

Vida let off rounds.

Agents were shooting at them from all directions.

Monique took off running across the lobby, screaming at the top of her lungs.

Firing her Glock, Vida caught the door and backed inside as bullets flew by her and crashed through the glass.

Tia continued firing as she dashed inside the building. A bullet slammed into her side just as she made it through the door. "AHHH!" she screamed out as she, Vida and Monique made a run for the stairs.

Agents rushed the building but found themselves locked out for a moment. And although bullets had done damage to the glass door, they still could not get through.

Tia yelled, "I'm hit!"

The Trio was now on the floor, at the door of the apartment that was in Baron's name. Police sirens were blaring outside.

Monique was so hysterical she couldn't get the key into the hole to open the door.

"Oh my God! Oh my God! What the hell is going on?!"

Vida snatched the key from Monique and opened the door. They all rushed inside the apartment, knowing they were trapped inside the building at this point.

Tia went straight to the ground from the pain of the bullet wound. She was bleeding dark blood that had the whole left side of her white Gap T-shirt soaked. "Fuck!" she shouted, rolling onto her back.

Vida knelt beside her and said, "Let me see how it looks." She pulled Tia's T-shirt up and saw the blood gushing out. "Damn!"

Monique was in a state of panic, looking out the window at all the law enforcement down on the street below.

"Oh my God, we're going to jail. It's thousands of cops outside. Why the hell did you shoot at them? What the hell do they want with you two? What are we going to do?" She threw countless questions in the air.

Vida snapped. "Shut up! Shut the fuck up and get me a wet towel!"

Monique jumped when Vida shouted and dashed to the bathroom.

Tia moaned in pain and gripped her Glock tightly.

"It's burnin', Vee. Gggggrrrrhhhh…Shit…" She gritted her teeth.

Glock in hand and tears in her eyes as she looked down at Tia, Vida knew the end was near. There would be no getting away this time. She shook her head and said, "Hold on, Tee. Just hold on."

Tia smiled painfully. "This is it, Vee. They got us cornered."

Monique returned with the towel and gave it to Vida. Vida applied pressure to Tia's gunshot wound to slow down the bleeding.

Monique went back to the window. "They got a fuckin' SWAT team out there now." Her cell phone went off. She answered it. It was FBI agent Brewer, he wanted to speak to Vida or Tia. Monique looked at Vida and handed her the phone without a word.

"Who is this?" Vida asked.

"Agent Brewer of the FBI, I want to give you and your two friends a chance to come out before it gets worse. It's over. If the SWAT team comes in, nobody comes out alive. We don't-" Vida hung up the phone.

Tia was sweating now. Death was close.

"What's up, Vee?" She said.

"They want us to come out and surrender."

"Fuck that," Tia shook her head against it. "We already said we ain't goin' alive. It's 'til death do us part, Vee. We ain't goin' back to the U.S. in cuffs. That's out."

"What about me?" Monique asked. "I don't have shit to do with what's going on."

Vida looked at Tia and said, "That's right she ain't got nothin' to do wit' this."

"Let her go." Tia said. "Tell 'em she coming out."

Vida nodded at Monique and said, "Hit'em back, tell 'em you comin' out."

Monique picked up the cell phone and pushed a button to call the last number back.

"I'm coming out, I don't have nothing to do with what's going on." She told the agent.

"What about the other two?" He asked.

"I don't know, but don't shoot me!" Monique shouted. She could hear agents in the hall outside of the apartment. "Let them know I'm coming out."

"I'll do that but let me speak to one of the other girls."

Monique handed Vida the phone.

"What!" Vida said as she slid a fresh clip in her Glock. Tia was doing the same.

The agent said, "We're going to let your friend come out unharmed. Once she's out, nice and safe, we're going to give you and your other friend a chance to come out the same way."

"Yeah, whatever." Vida said as she hung up and cocked her Glock.

"Baron is in the car with the cops!" Monique shouted with surprise.

Vida shook her head.

Tia smiled. "That nigga fuckin' wit' the law, he set us up."

Vida didn't care. "Go ahead on out, Monique." She told her.

"Help me up, Vee." Vida helped Tia to her feet. They were ready to fight to the death.

Monique was so nervous that she was shaking as she walked to the door and looked through the peephole. The hallway looked empty but she knew it wasn't. She looked back at Vida and Tia and felt sorry for them. Opening the door she stepped into the hallway with her hands in the air. Members of the SWAT team were posted at both ends of the hallway in helmets, vests, and armed with machine guns. They were ready to kill.

One of the SWAT members called out to Monique, "Walk slowly! Keep your hands in the air!"

Back inside the apartment, time was running out for Vida and Tia.

Tia looked out the window down on the crowded streets. News crews were already on the scene. A white sheet was over the body of one of the agents that Tia had smoked.

"It looks like they got a whole fuckin' army out here for little 'ole us."

Vida was sitting on the sofa with her head down holding her Glock with both hands. Her whole life was flashing before her eyes. The walls were closing in.

The cell phone rang again.

Tia looked at the phone and said, "Ain't shit else to talk about."

Vida took a deep breath. "You right, let's get this shit over wit'" She stood up and walked over to Tia and gave her a hug. "I love you, Tee. I love you so much." Tears filled Vida's eyes but didn't fall.

Tia held Vida tight. I love you too, boo."

"I'm so sorry 'bout all of this." Tears now ran down Vida's face.

"Ain't nothin' to be sorry for, Vee. This shit ain't your fault."

A loud bang at the door scared them and made them jump. Their hearts were already pounding and fear had numbed them. More banging on the door let them know that the SWAT team was right outside the apartment. Someone shouted, "This is your last chance!"

Vida and Tia let each other go and aimed their Glocks at the door.

Cutting her eyes at Vida, Tia said, "Let's go out wit' a bang."

Vida nodded, gripping her Glock with both hands. "Til death do us part!"

Another loud bang at the door and it flew open. All hell broke loose as gunfire tore through the small apartment. Vida and Tia lit the first one through the door and kept blasting as bullets tore through their bodies and knocked them to the floor.

Moments later, as the smoke cleared, FBI agent Brewer stepped into the apartment and saw the bloody bodies of Vida and Tia slumped and twisted on the floor. The apartment was destroyed. It smelled like tons of gunpowder and bullet holes were everywhere. Standing over the bodies he looked down and shook his head with pity. All he managed to say was, "Hell Razor Honeys."

The Cartel Collection
Established in January 2008
We're growing stronger by the month!!!
www.thecartelpublications.com

Cartel Publications Order Form
Inmates ONLY get novels for $10.00 per book!

Titles	*Fee*
Shyt List _____	$15.00
Shyt List 2 _____	$15.00
Pitbulls In A Skirt _____	$15.00
Pitbulls In A Skirt 2 _____	$15.00
Victoria's Secret _____	$15.00
Poison _____	$15.00
Poison 2 _____	$15.00
Hell Razor Honeys _____	$15.00
Hell Razor Honeys 2 _____	$15.00
A Hustler's Son 2 _____	$15.00
Black And Ugly As Ever _____	$15.00
Year of The Crack Mom _____	$15.00
The Face That Launched a Thousand Bullets	
_____	$15.00
The Unusual Suspects _____	$15.00
Miss Wayne & The Queens of DC	
_____	$15.00
Year of The Crack Mom _____	$15.00
Familia Divided _____	$15.00
Shyt List III _____	$15.00
Raunchy _____	$15.00
Reversed _____	$15.00

Please add $2.00 per book for shipping and handling.
The Cartel Publications * P.O. Box 486 * Owings Mills * MD * 21117

Name: _____

Address:_____

City/State:_____

Contact # & Email:_____

Please allow 5-7 business days for delivery. The Cartel is not responsible for prison orders rejected.

THE
CARTEL
street team
makin' this shit look too good...
Wanna earn some extra cash?
Join our street team and find out how?
Visit: www.thecartelpublications.com for more information.